Ariadne

Ariadne

Mike Gutowski

Mike Gutowski

For permission requests, contact the publisher, at:

Email: dadx3g@msn.com

Twitter: Mike Gutowski (@dadx3gMike) / Twitter

Facebook: https://www.facebook.com/ mike.gutowski.62

Instagram: www.instagram.com/ mike.gutowski.62/

Word Press: cratchandothernovels-bymikegutowski.com

Printed in the United States of America

ISBN: 978-1-7333895-2-5

eBook ISBN: 978-1-7333895-3-2

1. Dystopian Fiction. 2. Science Fiction. 3. Dark Fantasy.

First Edition

Let Forgiveness Reign Supreme.

"Zorya Polunochnaya is the sun's secret lover: she is the reason he returns home at the end of each day. After the sun sets, he retires to Zorya

Polunochnaya's bed. Every night he dies orgasmically in her arms, but each morning she revives him so the sun can once again ride through the sky."

The Encyclopedia of Spirits: The Ultimate Guide to the Magic of Fairies, Genies, Demons, Ghosts, and Goddesses, by Judika Illes, page 1037

Author's Note

Linguistics in this narrative are modeled on Ariadne's home planetoid language system. It has been translated into prevalent vernacular of the known humanoid world. An effort to maintain a familiar vernacular, yet not distance story essence from Ariadne's dialectical nuances, commences in kind.

1

From small points evolved Universes. Life existed imperfect. Intended imperfect. Still, there existed no coincidence. Technology assured such atonement.

Everything about Ariadne seemed ensnared in trap of past, present, and future. Sometimes, swirled soup of varied temperatures and delicate textures tickled spoon. Governments had become gods.

As youngling, Ariadne soon learned there existed no unintended creations or consequences in this Dimension Black Hole. Clearly determined math if not always path on planetoid Nazran. Only intended constructions persisted.

I relate, as Nazran Chronicler for Historical

Record, this Button Hand's Mission progress, as my First Draft submission, approval pending Final Controller review.

Ariadne's Mission story commenced as follows in telling I can best manage. Consulted Documentation included Training Machine Notes, Personal downloaded cognitive Diary, and Synched Button Hand microscopic memory chips incorporated into biology during Training. Such chips, we've learned, had become common in most worlds

of all known Dimensions, common as dust and products

biological, chemical, or inanimate. Mission world locales were evidence-tagged environments. Element Tagging served as reliable accountability measure to monitor Citizen responsibility Service.

All thoughts and actions in worlds centuries ago were tele-waved using microscopic receptor chips to sync humanoids, creatures, objects. My duty was to Catalogue all required evidence documents per Button Hand performance protocols. No action, no thought, no evidence was allowed to escape documentation process. All Elements accounted for, to date.

Ariadne Training

Ariadne's Button Hand Training experiences numbered Instructional Seminars. Some trials of varied complexity, and some errors designed as test experimentations; others flayed sentience material matters such as telekinetic abilities Ariadne greatly enjoyed in practice as amusement. Laughed inside, Ariadne did, at memory of Instructor named Flux who called Ariadne "my budding teek". His sage advice stuck to Ariadne's psyche in glue fashion. "Never become embroiled in another's self-served expedience. Never. It is disaster waiting to deviously unfold."

At proper age and Training Level attainment, Ariadne's programed Assignments proceeded in contained environment. Success Level of results determined further Assignment attractions. Little time for gloats or cheers.

Flux never hesitated to remind, "It is when dreams cross threshold into reality that real nightmares begin."

Each Assignment Post, every Mission targeted,

required positive results. Button Hands became disappeared almost regularly, sometimes conveniently, or were rumored so at Lower Class Levels from whence Ariadne originated. Fear nudged. Ariadne now served Overseer who served Controller who served Ordinator. All as means to serve self.

Almost into stasis, Ariadne fell. Awaited next progression of Mission Training session material. It grinded away in load status. Mud-cocked meanings peeked and pinched meekly at thoughts as Ariadne pulled back hammer of Analytics upsurge. Tried to dodge them. Sparks of such mental fire caused temporary awareness debilitation. Unusual wait time. End, Ariadne wished. End already, Ariadne pleaded. Quantum serial waves disconnection loomed, otherwise. Meant interminable darkness, Ariadne thought, yet not such bad result, for comfort concerns. Further thoughts projectiles stimulated no effect.

Ariadne tapped upper manus digits onto table. Stretched spinal canal. Ordered discs. Re-animated musculature elements. Stretched ligaments in search of moment's comfort. Silence screamed. Ariadne looked at self, realized primary gender designation needed. Tested "female" biological persona designation since performance goals aligned generally to assigned Mission Task responsibilities.

Suffered voids as chronological age changed appearance, but planned moments helped serve goals in conjunction with mindset. Unrested mind more dangerous than exhausted body. To self-extinguish was crime worse than Mission failure. Perhaps test of stamina, all this.

Room light changed from dark to light to searing, blinding single ray. Birthed androgynous, she had to choose her first Mission persona identity. Basic female attributes she modeled, but if necessary, later she could transform outward appearance to mimic male persona.

Training commenced in all these illumination ranges. She

liked dark best. Luxury, dark was, to her. Nurtured inside some mysterious place. Soothing calm comfort blanket. Finally.

Translation Choice: Humanoid Languages
Spool: X923876269
Cart Level: Sentient Synoptics
Interpretation Analytics: _______________

Confused as to this last option. Complete understanding of Target dimension world essential for Mission success. Perhaps this choice option bugged Training system. Further test of skills? She made vague her choice.

Interpretation Analytics: Tapered. Know more, Soft

Soft provided more flexibility to incorporate errors and misunderstood correlation to Target goals. She realized wider error range formula created greater risk in Mission completion. Details devils regularly haunted her thoughts. Perhaps test of Analytics ability.

Her perception also indicated wider error range created better opportunity for discovery of threats yet to be revealed, ever. Such sentience was not her primary goal, Mission aligned or otherwise, yet gnawed at her inner mind. Questions tortured certainty senses. Also created higher self-termination degrees, result from which recovery was not guaranteed. At least, if she survived, reward compensation became enhanced. Better food.

No one chose Soft on first Mission, at least, shared scuttlebutt revealed. She assumed such risk.

If she survived her Mission, future Button Hands could benefit from her results if declassification format authorized. Scuttlebutt secrets she deemed worthy target triggers. Brilliant minds miss nuances. Nuances. Ghosts of regret. "No one makes this choice," she thought aloud. Checked Training Results of prior Button Hands.

Training Results: Termination

Anomalies: Classified

Nerves tweaked, again. Reluctant, suspicious to yet reach conclusory observations, she checked for exceptions. Search sounds oozed from machined parts. "Machines were sentient beings, too," she guessed. Motor heart. Oil blood. Computer brains. She liked old humanoid terms applied to life structures. Helped her to understand humanoid Tech.

Such thought dots comforted her, for now. "Well, at least

someone else exploited possibilities." About to take break and stretch when strange symbols flooded screen, then coalesced into one word.

"Gomwind."

She did not understand. No question had she asked. Perhaps her last unanswered question finally resolved. She continued knowledge scan under "Gomwind".

Result: Gomwind

Apparently, she accidentally discovered channel outside Training Session material, still suspicious whether method or maelstrom triggered findings. Intent purposeful, more likely. Perception hunts became tortured trails.

Author: Classified

Data Quality: Ambient

Reliability: In progress

Knowledge Form: Narration

Source: Praetorius Class RID Tracker

Readability Status: Loading

"Ugh," she thought. Her digital appendages entered dual source search. "Now driving off-road path," thoughts punched her. Silence mind clicks breached each of her brain stems. Darkness thoughts began assault. Shadows loomed over. Escape. Escape. Random thoughts permeated. She worried. Deceit harbingers cooed at her incessantly. "Boymore" word poked at her side vision. Glanced at screen, she did, but such word did not present there, on screen. "Glitch poke," she guessed. "Boymore?" No such entity exists, she reminded herself. At least, she had not encountered anatomy or biology of such creature.

Sub-Search: RID

"Readiness In Demand" trackers known to be notoriously errant and stale in usefulness. Named after famous Nazran data seeker who eventually disappeared.

"Disappeared usually meant never seen again but could mean otherwise," she hoped. Prior knowledge perceptions told her to interpret this data as "Laying low", or perhaps "Renamed", then reassigned to protect identity.

More data spilled forth from search. She eyed result.

"Presumed dead after thousand years and such time had long passed."

The Machine seemed to be talking to her. Not in sound waves but in thought waves. Secrecy path she had fallen upon. Still, she needed some clues in event Gomwind encounters happened. She had forgotten what RID meant in detail but remembered it was not to be ignored information. Significant. Popped up near Training list top for reason important. Readiness void forged assured track towards extermination if she did not proceed on this path

further. Report Summary unfolded accordingly.

"Two Jorsons, Frakker and Jentsen, made their way along asphalt road. Just another day almost turned into evening along way of what is moment's journey and jewel. In their world, time had no constraints. Only moments ruled. Each moment appeared, built upon itself, continued into another moment of unknown to be determined time, or not. Just blackness, void, silence reigned, or not. Only temperate certainty existed to grasp wild reins of uncertainty. But if moment meaning revealed itself, and purpose arose from dim Starizon, an enlightening revelation rain boded hope, should such necessary deeds become recognized, carried out, completed. But whim like wind interceded regularly. Species characters and creatures popped in and out and changed destinies.

To make sense of it all was foolishness. As such, religion was born in this course of thinking. Do not try to figure out what cannot be. If such thought gave way to another more subtle thread of meaning, so be it if last religion vanquished itself from memory. Survival was rule, meaning, purpose. Why survival was so important no one knew. Old trope debunked in ancient history of more sentient dimensions. Perhaps selfish it seemed to those not nuanced in intricacies of perspective attached to an individual's personal experience, culture, or traditionalistic ingrained rituals, but such thinking ruled every societal setting. It always was and always would be, until it was not anymore either naturally or otherwise.

Weather was demi-god. Ruled days and nights which were decided by odd randomness. No way to figure it out yet. Starizon Masters tried to figure out such circumstances, whether regular or irregular, normal or strange, but too many dark spots in heavens to calculate. So, must be prepared, all. Educated, all, as best as possible. At least, enough to distinguish between fungible tripe and truth, or perish so. More sentient civilizations had allowed gods' worship to slip into oblivion, yet round and around, governments again became gods.

Either path failed to rescind ultimate moral

decay. Such strange world of unpredictable it was that outsiders learned to rarely visit as they learned they could be perceived in many ways: invaders, visitors, helpers, scholars, trespassers, gods, or even food. Helpers were most dangerous of these. Never one came in peace. Came only to get their piece of pie. What was known bred danger. What was unknown bred ignorance. Such poisons proved equally fatalistic.

Foreign concept peace remained. Survival meant quick assessment of things and those unknown, and even quicker action upon, after interpretation of projected or perceived sentiments and intentions. To be mistaken about such was not crime or sin as survival excused all. Survival was judge. No such ideas as good or evil, evil or good, evil, or good evil were allowed or tolerated, at least, until reckoning day. Be or not to be only ruled. Each concept could change at sound of ricket's chirp.

Such were Gomwind rules. Rugged and harsh were these rules to outsiders. Outsiders never lasted long. Their weapons were useless. Beings and living entities of Gomwind evolved into super bugs, near indestructible. Skin, organs, appendages, each connected to central power source of planetary system in which it existed. All elements of Universe somehow combined into this system. An unknown source energy converted all elements into an only strongest survive living entity or being. Death did not exist. Only transformation existed. Outsiders had no such abilities or evolutionary systems at their disposal, as far as Gomwinds were aware.

Gomwinds of Gomwind were essentially invincible. Outsiders many times came to discover secrets of Gomwind, but there were not secrets from Gomwinds' perspectives. All was all and none was none. No in between. It was doll's life. Useful, not useful, never disposed, only ignored. If their home world Dimension, Starizon, intact existed, then no changes nor outsiders' visits could extinguish it. The world of worlds it was and be all and end all of existence. Not that there was some predictability after Eons of evolution on Gomwind. Unpredictability determined greatest strength. Energy source of Gomwind still remained relatively unknown and uncharted information piece in science and history logs of off worlds.

All Gomwinds' knowledge was biologically

shared through genetic transference. All disease was eradicated in same way. No families existed or needed. No relationships or societies necessary. Each living entity could choose form, shape, purpose, need, desire, actions. Each free to act or not, exist or not, although to choose not boarded temporary choice, regardless of how many Eons passed. Gomwinds resurrected forever.

Where origination of such thoughts came from ruled common Gomwind questions. Years could be used to figure out answer, which became unturned lily pads, mind dagger's of unanswered questions. Gomwinds did not care much about time, as such thought long ago became unnecessary. Time was commodity. Life and death thoughts did not exist either. Gomwinds eternal lived. Their life forms could stop in function, during stasis evolution, but such time point stood temporary, even if long in time passing, until another moment exploded them back onto scene of planetoid Gomwind in Dimension Starizon. Yes, redundancy in evolution. Of necessity in such culture. Repetition led to excellence, and excellence to supremacy.

Highest form of Gomwind existence mastered

stasis time, so it became almost non-existent. Only Gomwinds who mastered knowledger analytics could do such to and for themselves. Highest life craft form neared instantaneous reincarnation, and no loss of prior gained knowledge in skill resulted amid process."

Ariadne alighted from her resting position. Ensued then, some unplanned rumination. Shrouded in thought, escape not option. Machine noise alerted her to more information formulated. Origin Request processing, she determined from machine sounds. Further enlightenment awaited introduction to her. Jorsons as Gomwind history keepers melded into Gomwind culture, only to disappear as separate species. That, she learned, and Gomwind existence reason.

Translation Choice: Subject Origin
Spool: Z676767130D13
Cart Level: Clan Affiliation
Interpretation Analytics: Ariadne

"What?" Her brains sparked, confused. She did not ask questions about herself. Never occurred to her in thoughts. Apparently, her Personnel file, not permitted for her own personal perusal, began to appear. More data churned outward, almost in melodic march-step tunes.

Origin Species: Oni Clan

Origin Sub-Species: Gomwind Clan

Confused, she became. She was physically tall enough to satisfy Gomwind genetics parameters. Yet, too small overall she stood for classification in Oni lore. Given Oni culture classified as myth more than historical fact, her primary classification rang even more curious. Someone in Overseer ranks must have been pranking her. Perhaps intentional false flag to test her wits.

She brushed off distressed thoughts. Looked at Machine screen again. Not sure why, but small numbers jiggled at lower left. Never gave them much attention, until now. Seems tomorrow had arrived. Date shook her. Days passed by while not attracting her attention. Many days, it appeared. Many.

Ariadne realized Ordinator who pushed her Controller and Overseer also influenced Universes and interlocked Dimensions thereof. Perhaps Ordinator was Gomwind in origin. Her thoughts did not allow time fluctuation for such fantastical wisdom philosophy. To realize an understanding that unknown existed in no finite terms provided enough curiosity to seek answers.

Such flighty conclusion encounters further disturbed her. Did not need Controller's heaped-upon enmity. Still, it served as boundary barrier. Some educated comfort there. Do not go where they will not go, intellectually, meant haven, for now. Machine screen went blank. Lessons over. Rumination ensued. She realized sedentary regimen of Training stimulated physical needs neglected. Her numerous limbs she stretched, detached some, and flexed each in multiple rhythms.

She hoped this effort was not another caustic Research Drop, a Sub-Category which many times lead to nowhere, yet would eventually become needed, if not now, for this Mission, or later.

Search: Oni

Origin Source: Old Earth Domain, Humanoid Realm

Resource Identity: Ranker, Graveyard Shift

Topic: Religious Differences

Research Link: https://www.ranker.com/

list/buddhism-monsters-and-demons/edira-putri?ref=rltdlsts_collection

"Oni are ogre-like demons from Japanese Buddhism. Depicted as horrendous, giant beasts, Oni have brightly colored skin (usually blue or red), different numbers of horns, toes, fingers, and sometimes eyes. They wield massive iron clubs (kanabo), and their spirits are reborn from dead souls with an ax to grind – those who perished in famines or epidemics, jealous women, or wicked people condemned to a tormented afterlife in a Buddhist hell. They dole out punishment to wicked people and serve the demon lord Enma.'

'The powers of the Oni are tremendous – they can reattach body parts they lose in fights, fly, change form at will, and inflict disease, insanity, and death as they see fit. Intelligent and extremely nasty, Oni revel in causing societal breakdown, and eat and drink to excess. Their favorite food is human flesh."

"Must I die to understand death?" Ariadne wondered. She anticipated "Yes" answer from Ordinator tasked to manage her Controller. She risked punishment if Training failed her. Who pushes who, determines who falls. Such questions escaped answers except in near-death Training session experiences.

Only one answer resulted. Shame. Shame to her. Shame to her Controller. Pressing enforcement of such predicament risks fell primarily upon her. Corollary dissension risked blow back even more onerous. So long as curiosity existed in her determined self, continuation of Training elements served soothingly as thirst quencher.

Numerous thoughts plagued her duality brain during Training sessions. Anatomy familiarity still eluded complete mastery for her. Six long appendages above body mid center allowed for multiple maneuvers of swift strike, and room for error. Three appendages below mid center enabled tree root stability even on slippery surfaces.

To understand herself always marked first Task, in any situation. Golden rule sting. Remember, then remember again. Strength. Weakness. Compensate. Overestimate. Underestimate. Fate swaths stung hard in either direction.

She remembered odd events as youngling. Whispered concerns emanated from Elders around her.

Curious looks hovered amidst her walk, talk, contemplation moments, as if others wondered about or feared her thoughts. Paranoia was diagnosis. Excessive levels. Needed to be reined in or useless her existence became. So too, talk of her initial generation survival was debated. Too soon and too much sentience level. Outside curve of predicted evolutionary parameters.

Erratic possibilities only resulted from such births. Such

entities, talents and weakness potentials unknown, created fear in Ordinator circles. One significant mistake by single Button Hand risked species extermination. Perhaps what was new in some Dimension worlds was old in others. Perception point earned. Worth effort.

3

2

"Oops." She forgot to practice her Assignment appearance. Required daily per Training routine. She flowed over towards changing room, deep inside masking wardrobe. Located wig. Placed on head using one tentacle. Adjusted with another tentacle. Rotated eyes outward and around her head to determine proper convexity in relation to head shape. Removed wig. She would have to make quick adjustments at Mission site destination, depending on societal observations. Located hair pill pod, ingested, practiced hair growth. "Nice," she thought.

Information systems for her destination were somewhat sparse. Location had recently drawn notice for many disturbances. Part of Mission required she glean further data for analysis relevant to future potential Missions. Mission review materials, for now, relevant.

She loaded next Training Session, but system still stuck on Background review. Garbled symbols popped on screen. System emanated low-level crunch sounds, almost guttural in nature. Soothing, to her audible receptors.

Source: Timesitter

Identity: Terry Gruesome, alias Mee

Accessory: Dog named June

Communication: from Journal Entries

Era Date: Classified.

She requested more data.

Define: Timesitter

"A global Timesitter is like babysitter, except baby is 'time'; uses time to get what info Overlords want."

"Methods: Arrange time and circumstance to set up revelations or deceits for designated character subjects to 'discover', then act upon. Sometimes Timesitter starts gossip, or causes physical incidents to occur, or makes things look different than actual perspective. Effort goals not to change, but more like regulate."

Report Summary commenced.

" 'Come on, June. We gotta' get goin' on this one. Gotta' give the State what they paid us for. But you know my mantra. Give 'em more than they pay for. Never know. They might go lookin' for someone else. Then where would we be. Eatin' garbage scraps most likely.'

Mee existed as a Timesitter, descended from eons of Timesitters. He learned the skills at his father's knee and his grandfather's hip. June stopped licking himself. He looked up at Mee. Toughest part of the job was not doing it. Toughest part was keeping up with Rules. They changed regularly. In Mee's view, not because it made job easier or more efficient, but because it gave Controller more power. They were not smarter, or faster, or better. Controllers' primary credential: they were related to extant Controllers as sons, daughters, or some such biological connection.

Part One

Timesitter conducted one of his missions which demonstrated his authority, powers, and results.

Reported back to Overlords. Punished. Reason: overachieved, which at his Level was near sinful given it meant his Overseer was wrong about this Timesitter's potential and developed skill set. Punishment afforded to Overseer considered destructive in hierarchy culture, so instead, Timesitter was castigated. Food ration reduced.

In one example case, Mee held an elevator he knew would fail for someone who needed to be injured, to give an opportunity for someone else to take over the injured persons job.

Part Two

Timesitter learned during next mission, the repugnant repercussions for citizens squashed under thumbs of Overlords, then developed somewhat of a conscience sentience, rather unexpectedly. Did not understand why it was happening to him. At Tavern on rest stop, after observations catalogued, Timesitter loosely spoke about his concerns and reservations. Conversation overheard by nearby patron who reported it to authorities. Were Overlords using another Timesitter to set him up for failure?

Part Three

Timesitter reeked revenge, or activities so described in such manner, on Overlords, by using an interpretation of their demands against them. No example provided."

Ariadne's research interrupted by Warning message pop up while she wondered whatever happened to June. She wondered, too, what words "a" and "the" meant. Waste.

Sync: Caution

"Do not undergo transformation after Planetoid's sun rise until day (language interpretation in progress) light or until time conjunction exceeds 50 percent quadrant of day light cycle. Self-emollition could ensue."

She read words again. Again, she read. One more time to synchronize this thought into memory. She knew self-emollition recovery time would end her Mission goals and create failure scenario to unfold. She wondered if perhaps another Mission opportunity would manifest itself upon her being in event of such blunder. "Must remember."

Next issue begged for attention. She could not help but notice dialectical oddities in Summary description. Maybe source sprung from humanoid ancestry. Failure scenario still intrigued. Perhaps she would become beneficiary of another evolution opportunity. Start from scratch. Grow again. Evolve into stronger entity. Only allowed if some new insight gained, or one merited as worthy pursuit by Controllers, or moments showed themselves in revelatory manner, if her contributions were not erased and credited solely to Controllers' Group. She feared such circumstances more than termination.

Session stalled again, almost as if unseen hand presented additional data sources not previously permitted to this knowledge scheme. Pop. Pop.

Subject: Skinner's Folly

Identity: Doctor Skinner

Communication: Classified

Era Date: Classified.

Report: See Summary.

Skinner's Folly Summary

Scientist named Skinner experimented in DNA acceleration. Tried to speed up humanoid evolution in effort to determine if more prefect and wholesome humanoids could achieve this type of sentient existence. He experimented with known

DNA strands to determine what may have been missed or discarded or overlooked in perspective views. Managed to increase DNA evolution by incredible speed mathematically.

He began to wonder if he was an inter-dimensional being. His vision, his perspective was much stronger than average humanoid vision. His instruments of investigation were not common to humanoid instrumentation known during this categorized time Era.

One of his instruments enabled sight of third DNA strand in previously known two-strand DNA sequencing code, undetectable by humanoid instruments previously. In code, he sequenced out strands indicative of unusual peaceful and calm humanoid beings. He then ran through known databases and developed no findings.

Dormant code shrouded in mystery. Either never discovered previously, or discovered and knowledge discarded, or monopolized by those who craved power and control to dominate all other living and unliving, sentient and non-sentient species lines.

Essentially, he had discovered beings otherwise

unknown in catalogued humanoid histories. He named them "Sounders" and further, defined them as glue that held together all sentient beings. Glimmer of hope he developed philosophically at this discovery. He theorized Sounders still existed, of necessity in secret, to weave threads of calm, hope, perhaps in religious presence; as buoy, or threads woven universally as means to hold all existence together.

When his theory was finally reviewed, skepticism and perhaps jealousy emerged among mentors and associates. His career essentially ended under burden of social scorn. In his scholarly world, no such creature traits were considered natural traits of existence, either relevant, or certainly not essential. Tribalism, conquest for resources acquisition, subjugation for economic benefit ruled societal institutions just as plagues leveled natural and known fields of humanoid existence.

Ariadne wondered if she was of Sounder etiology also, or at least, distant relative of such humanoid culture. She could not recall too many instances of rage or outrage in any moments of her own existence. Frustration, yes. Disgust, yes.

Perhaps Skinner identified himself as first discovered Sounder.

Summary of tech toys: flying cars, flying drones, 3-D printers printing of virtually anything including humanoid body or creature body internal and external organs, self-driving cars, flying suit jet packs for atmosphere and beyond flying, bendable mobile phone screens, android dogs, cashier-less stores, virtual reality (travel world w/o leaving couch), robot companions, refrigerators you can talk to, electronic money. Many of these devices evolved into biological or chemical attachments to humanoid anatomy either by mechanical, construct, or synthetic or microchip absorption. Nothing free. Higher humanoid culture Classes acquired more refined tech elements available.

She wondered whether species crossbreeding, now outlawed, existed in past so distant, all crossbreds were now extinct. Perhaps there were exceptions, for Elite beings, or maybe it was phased out over time and some crossbreds remained, even after hundreds or thousands of years; or perhaps lesser beings ignored such rules. Lesser beings greatly outnumbered elite beings Dimension-wide.

Define: Elite Class beings

Perhaps Elitism was disease, of mind and soul. To beat disease, one had to "be at" it, that is, use body as shield and use body in measured course of actions for attack ruled by mind impulses. Such bodies and minds tended to become controlled by Elemental Spirits. Were such entities "Sounders"? Unfortunately, her Training only provided cursory review time of this subject. She had meant to get back to it for more information but made determination it likely would not become a factor in her initial Missions. She saved source for future reference.

Source Save: https://paranormalschool.com/elemental-spirits-complete-guide/

Breeding methods tempted investigation into her mind. How to find, quickly, secretly, she wondered. Mating knowledge could be useful for traps to lay upon Mission Targets.

Gomwind sex involved bit of dance, body exploration as female hid entry amidst varied body forms. Female body became map exploration, hinted at routes, some which became necessary dead ends to achieve maximum productivity efforts from partner explorer. Partner matches mattered not, except for evolution continuation.

In many species, evolution continuation did not remain supreme. Pleasure reigned supreme, perhaps due to less necessary reproduction needs. Over and under population cyclical resulted, sometimes driven by need, sometimes ridden by emotion. Most productive explorer rewarded in kind. No practice had she in these potentially helpful trapping endeavors.

Scientist Skinner species: Trivarian (dual brains, two stems)

Trivarian biology and etiology mimicked some of other advanced species known, but knowledge revelations were infinite. Surprises existed, unpleasant and otherwise.

Now she wondered even more about her own etiology. Oni? Gomwind? Sounder? Trivarian? Mix of all four into one, like her bilateral brain itself? Somewhat made sense if there existed connection between brain development and genetic history. How many like her? Needless concern, she told herself. Still, curious to find someone like one of her ancestral breeds. Such luxury not available to her purpose. She digested source info further.

"Skinner started by testing on microscopic elements, like amoebas, then advanced to varied (mainly Earth Dome, for cost reasons) insect species, mice, rats, frogs, rabbits, then humanoids of varied Dimension cultures who volunteered. Transportation costs were high in newly developed cargo shuttle systems. Generally, humanoids of no specific physical residence domain who searched for safe-haven food sources and places to reside were legion. Skinner owned much land. Installed housing locations. Utilized cameras for video and audio monitoring.

Skinner liked pizza, unusual toppings, ordered from same

nearby food source and requested carryout delivery. Pizza humanoid worker, college student working part-time usually delivered on late-night shift. Student became overtly curious as his college study concentrated on Astrobiology. Student was also avid follower of UFO history and had developed his own theory of UII.

Skinner referenced UII in his research notes: Unidentified Interdimensional Identification. It was his belief that extra-terrestrials were not regularly visiting from outer space, but rather from inner space through Dimension doors connected to vortex tunnels filled by unknown element substances or gases which allowed seamless transport from one Dimension to another.

Seamless, not so much, as some beings were split during travel, perhaps inadvertently, which resulted in existence simultaneously among at least two Dimensions, and not necessarily in same physical form, yet still in one single sentience form. Such beings were unable to communicate across Dimensions.

Skinner retained his gender designation of "he" as means to attract all genders. To not identify risked apprehension among those identified and claimed. He eventually learned some humanoid cultures had discarded gender designations as they biologically evolved into multiple gender anatomy. He also learned lesser sentient creatures had evolved into genderless form as means to survive.

Biological gender change needs were required

at any time depending on species necessities, as evidenced by marine, plant and other land-based populations including insect habitats, across all known Dimensions. Even these evolutionary feats failed to avoid extinction of most species throughout history.

He began to realize there were generations of inter-dimensional beings of many species classifications that inhabited Earth Dome. They had influenced history and development from microbiologic to macro-biologic forms. Such evidence still existed either in living matter or catalogues of previous such incarnations.

Eventually, Skinner lost control of his experiments but refused to admit errors, until new humanoid species inadvertently, he discovered: an inside out humanoid, of organs-maintained function outside endoskeleton. Outer skin not necessarily needed as internally fused body structure incorporated general surrounding micro-biology wrapped by translucent ecto-protective material. In such creatures, outer skin not considered essential except for cosmetic reasons. Skinner struggled to classify such finding.

Eventually, some homeless humanoids left lab village area housing, started attacking all living things around them. They formed clan-like packs, learned to hunt humanoids, animals, insects as prey."

What else could be expected in any species? Not question.

It was answer. Search for truth often sidelined and twisted by places sentient minds feared to travel. For lesser sentients, no such consideration needed. Survival first and last reigned. Methods not filtered by morals or creeds. Hogwozzled regularly by rumors and defamations. Advantages in either direction countered by varied complications. Some moralistic principles in themselves qualified as dangerous and specious predator Class traits. Fundamentals of any such altruistic machinations clung hinged upon purpose foundation breadth and strength. Sugar and spice and everything lethal rested, waited, on quivered haunches there.

In self-imposed and isolated retrospection mode, source of such thoughts she could not locate. Partition between brains she searched. No origin point located. Perhaps programmed subtly during Training Sessions. Too many questions, not enough answers. Status stabbed confidence quotient.

"Relax. Relax. Escape dubious thought batter," she self-counseled. Smokey paste of trance faded. Gray sentience comfort enveloped her. Searched minds for resolutions. One Old Earth poet's words slapped at her moment.

"Animals, we are in fits and starts. Trembling, shaking, breaking apart our deeds and tasks and moments of mark.

Sun is up, light adorns until Moon takes over to cover the

thorns. Once in bloom, twice in death, sleep and wake and

catch last breath.

Never done, the lonely one who brings and does, then quakes like rain. Give us time, we hope and dream, as again days' time rule shakes a stream.

Wait, one more moment, something needs done, yet rest

and hope beg sustenance again. Please give strength to at least seek fun.

No, no, seeking is for fools. Doing, making,

breaking is rule. Maybe, somehow, good result beams less cruel. Sacred are these, human toil and tool.

One day sunrise will break silent wild scattered skies and we devils devoid too late for a cry. Die, die ending blink of eyes.

No voices or sounds except what is left 'round. Break, break one more wave on the sound. Lighthouse no shine.

Boats broken, covered brine.

Deserts awake, at night minus day. Waiting, waiting, waiting away. Sun is up, light adorns until moonlight again covers the thorns."

Many questions thwacked at her after reading such words. Overwhelm media conglomerates, politicians, university professors, teachers, police, military installations, until new species evolved to hold onto land mass size of manageable territory? Reconfiguration of prevalent norms required to regenerate base principles of cultures.

She wondered if Skinner discovered extraterrestrial influence on humanoids of varied worlds and Dimensions. Autopsies and government investigations by Agencies unidentified by name were compromised to direct humanoid evolution direction. Were there competing Alien species exerting influence? Were Angels aliens? Were god stories and myths related to surveillance, then contact between humanoids and other aliens going back eons of humanoid and creature history? Aliens from one world were humanoids in another and likewise in reverse.

Search Machine spit out loosely related alternative data.

Result: Axolotl

Source: Old Earth Extant Records

References: https://www.nationalgeographic.com/animals/amphibians/a/axolotl/

https://www.msn.com/en-us/lifestyle/did-you-know/20-animals-you-never-knew-existed/ss-BB15FAMB?ocid=msedgntp#image=19

"Also known as the Mexican walking fish (Old Earth creature), this animal is in fact a salamander. Unlike other members of its species, the axolotl retains its dorsal fin and gills into adulthood. This is what is known as neoteny, meaning that they stay in their larval state without ever undergoing metamorphosis. The axolotl also has a superpower: it is able to regenerate damaged organs, from an eye to part of their brain. Found in Xochimilco Lake, Mexico, this remarkable creature unfortunately finds itself on the list of endangered species."

She wondered if Old Earth creature species DNA had been mined, then sold on open market to any interested other humanoid, alien, or creature culture. Tired, she coveted some mental solace, but again, Machine urged further music listening. Maybe review "Hell Meaning" course. Near Universal and Dimensional concepts for no certain reason she could discern. Must know more.

She learned Hell myths of various cultures. Cold as in "cold as hell". Read like, essentially, garbage dump description. Hell. Heaven. Such descriptions irritated her. How sentient, or not, some civilizations must be to rely on such myths for comfort. See it as it is, her thoughts prodded, and not as it is wished to be. As irritating as such myth accounts presented themselves to her, learn it she must, or die at hands of those who maniacally incorporated these thought patterns. Still, self-enslavement accomplished by such entity societies created much easier extinction moment to accomplish. Those who welcomed end of days were gratefully granted wish.

More Hell thoughts interjected. No micro-organisms

present to preserve flesh or organs against biological invaders. Slow, painful body rot steady marked course. Psychological pleasures became painful tortures of too needy nurture.

Can demons "borrow" time from their next, reincarnated life for use in current life? What if proved unable to pay such debt? Price for borrowing against subjugation to will of an Ordinator? Perhaps Hell analogy. Bitter taste, this subservience to one that dictates an Ordinator of conditions and guides to destinies. Someone had to do it. Not her. An Ordinator seemed someone much better to her mind. No concern now. Move on to know more. Always know more necessary. Break into unknown. Discover it. Define it. Corral it. Box it. Wrap it. Cage it. Head shake necessitated for escape from broken thought tracks. Endless searches stimulated her. Braking from course depressed.

Energy drain of process offered her temporary respite. Breathe. She sucked in as much atmosphere as able to experience temporary heights of high. Room instruments fluctuated. She relaxed to avoid energy disturbance of Training session. Did not want to shut down fun. Her Training sessions fell outside Program norms. Castigated for it in past. This game, this game, engaged. Loser died.

Manage it she could. Must learn more than they know. Must. Scared them, she realized. Already her Training Sessions red-marked up and down for excessive knowledge proliferation. Apparently disturbed her counterparts who could not manage similar stamina. Avoid confrontation. Controller advice she failed to appreciate. Learned how to walk that tightrope. Alternative resulted in detritus cleanup. Worthy profession. Not her goal. Her goal had no limits. Just needed to keep it boxed, secreted in her mind closet, or feathers ruffled nervous in higher Ranks. Edibles beckoned needs to her mind, body. Just little bit more knowledge. Just little.

More study beckoned. She shed some nearly microscopic tentacle portions as means to absorb some relaxation. Shards and tiny rolls floated then attached to porous and other surfaces and amused themselves while transmitting back to her some relief. Convenient and worthy little soldiers they were. They would return to her exosmic surfaces when entertainment became boredom, to provide analytical status of findings.

Next subject study. Omniverse. Plural Omniverses. Numbers of supposedly co-existing universes. See also multiverse. Purses of life, she thought. Omniverse is all things extant in any Dimension and Universe in entirety of existence. Beyond Omniverse. Omniverse exists in surrounding emptiness known as Outside, a void of virtual nothingness. Whatever may lie outside of these concepts is referred to Beyond, one of many iterations contained by Transcendentem. Tired eyes told her refuse to look up long big T word. Not going there. Discretion's valor stabbed at her back. Perhaps for next Mission study needed. Switched back to Hell study.

Descriptors. Grave, doom, corruption pit, underworld, clinging mud, shadow of death, valley, cauldron of God, fireplace, place of burning, place to be spit upon, destruction, ruin, silence, oblivion, cistern of sound, lowest earth, dividing curtain, place of destruction, loss, waste, serpents, dragons, place of future punishment. A place of no activity. Silence torture. No biological stimulation. Next word "medieval" escaped her mental grasp, but again, not interested so skipped its context. Medieval sources: 7 layers. Ho hum.

Some religious stuff peppered into mix. Baha's Faith: symbolic representations of spiritual conditions, closest to God is heaven, and conversely, remoteness from God is hell. Buddhism: 5 levels? Jainism, 7 grounds, lower part of

universe.

God, god, deity, Nod. "Narcissistic bastardy much?" She wondered. "Save souls or take over controls?"

What is Religion? Word religion comes from Latin word ligare: to join, or link, classically understood to mean linking of human and divine. What constitutes religion is subject to much dispute in field of theology and among ordinary people. "Too many words. Not enough meanings," she thought.

Someone appended description with Note: believing in

religion is like politics. Prepare to become

extremely disappointed. You will be castigated, ostracized, and in some cases killed politically, socially, and economically for disagreements. She did not care about politics. Did not think it would matter for her place in Universe. "Enough of this," her brains demanded.

Reading piqued her brain, or more grated upon it to point she drifted into self-absorption. Bored. She looked up her name. Simple attempt at purpose enlightenment. Ariadne means "most holy", composed of Cretan Greek elements "most" and (adnos) "holy". "Even my name has religious meaning in some humanoid cultures. Geesh."

She skimmed through to more source materials. Her primary understanding resulted in thoughts of whether she needed computer screen to learn story. She much preferred listening to dialect and words combinations. Switched to oral recitations. Moved her feet onto learning bench edge. Transferred muscle tissue and fat pads to back of head for relax mode. Soaked in knowledge; let it float about inside her brains; no prohibitions mode. Some few times, system re-routed from her question or thought conclusion. She did not resist.

Running out of time. Would figure it out later, she hoped hope of pretty presumption. Mind candy she appreciated, for now, until monumental moments might happen, in future, when confrontation required.

Screen kept blanking out. "Shite." She allowed this word

sound into her consciousness in swirl around and cleanse, as expression of consternation. Felt good, this vent. One word. Sweet mental relief. Mind toilet flush. "Hark back to, as needed." Repeated ad nauseum to remember. Museum of thoughts blotted her into submission. Succumb to it, she agreed to herself. Such personal negotiations soothed her minds.

Her name popped into mind again. Intrigued, she researched further. It appeared in Old Earth humanoid history under "Greek mythology".

Name Search, Enhanced: Ariadne

Daughter of King Minos. She fell in love with Theseus and helped him to escape Labyrinth and Minotaur but was later abandoned by him. Eventually she married god Dionysus. Ariadne, in Greek mythology, daughter of Pasiphae and Cretan King

Minos. She fell in love with Athenian hero Theseus and, with a thread or glittering jewels, helped him escape Labyrinth after he slew Minotaur, beast half bull and half man that Minos kept in Labyrinth.

Why did Theseus abandon Ariadne? Reason Theseus went to Crete could have been more for reason to get fame than to help Athens. When Theseus leaves Ariadne, she becomes fueled with anger and loneliness, which causes her to easily fall in love with Dionysus, mending broken heart she had because of Theseus.

"What's broken heart?" She allowed temporary wonderment to cloud burning thought pricks.

What is Dionysus most known for? Dionysus was ancient Greek god of wine, winemaking, grape cultivation, fertility, ritual madness, theater, and religious ecstasy. His Roman name was Bacchus. He may have been worshiped as early as 1500-11000 BCE by Mycenean Greeks.

Greek Deity Hyacinthus? She imagined herself as reference material. Ariadne is demon being, assigned to earth, to clean up some crime messes, perhaps caused by other demons who inhabited souls of evil humanoids or perhaps not humanoids but demons who wrongfully entered humanoid realm. Sure. She invented name for herself. Sedeathdress. She seduced humanoids, for price, to escape hell.

She entered question into Search Training, because mind begged for more knowledge, almost beyond her own control. Thought of this very moment scared her. Wondered, she did, if Machine was controlling her thoughts and Research travel path.

"What species connected to designated Dimension world environment relevant to Mission Tasks?" She waited. Waited more. Still more. Apparently, she stumbled on another system anomaly. System belched abject misery sounds, then data.

"Dark Matter is curtain between dimensions of universe, compartmentalizing it, to protect those behind curtain who utilize invention of artificial suns, and to protect Dark Matter dimension from discovery. . . ." Then Machine generated its own Search Data. Ugly, it sounded, like gears shredding, breaking, baking, raking.

Search: Relevant Reference Data
Source: Goth Literature
Sub-Set: Old Earth Domain

Result: https://penandthepad.com/10-elements-gothic-literature-8104633.html

"I guess my appearance screams Goth."

She thought for seconds. Skin cloth coverings allowed for concealment of physical appearance, and weapons implements. "I'll go with that." She especially liked head hood and near full body cloth cover. Black in color, to reduce reflection, and create shadow source creep curtain.

Search: Artificial Sun Source

Resource: Old Earth Domain

Result: https://www.bing.com/search?q=artificial+sun&form=EDGTCT&qs=PF&cvid=24fa683089a34d1f8c286e24aad77593&refig=7659b3c31d2d469af745481be52389d2&cc=US&setlang=en-US&elv=AXK1c4IvZoN-qPoPnS%21QRLOOeTklf-GQL%21EjAxC3nk0PScp9bCt8aMFSR5Wbpv6yUsGB6aDTKqOPy74toouogkyl4y5ipiQ7H1X*8jtPYVr0l5&plvar=0&PC=HCTS

She did not expect such output. System rebooted. Why

Old Earth resources peppered searches, she

pondered. Perhaps her Dimension destination resembled Old Earth social constructs. Many civilizations mirrored each other. New data showered from screen.

Mission Target Entities: Biological

Sub-Set: Humanoid

Ventnoirs: voracious eaters of mind and spirit, both literally and figuratively. Consumption of brains allowed incorporation and assimilation of victim's knowledge and experience. Essentially, users and takers and self-obsessed pariahs.

Hugwanes: able to hypnotize using scent on and of their victims. They copy scents and use as trails for victim attractions. Essence allowed mind control. Used to acquire wealth or any goods or services of target victim.

Essentially, magical thieves.

Corpolvanders: virtually unable to permanently die as they possessed powers of sequential revivals of their own souls. Powers used to provide favors to victims and in exchange, then accumulate reciprocal commitments from victims who become obligated to do their bidding. Essentially, elitists, or humanoids who think their shite does not stink.

Normals: most of primary humanoid population. Other beings listed above had migrated to this world over eons. Normals were aware of these off-world entities and attempted to steer clear, but it was difficult to identify off-world beings from Normals. Least able to resist temptations of more advanced humanoid specimens. Canonical injected mindsets instilled from birth to death allowed brief form of societal function protections for as long as Normals followed constructed community canon.

Crossovers: mongrels, mix of humanoid and other creature biology who adopted semi-independent mindset functions, then became summarily swallowed whole by one or more cultural morays. Essentially, mongrels functioned ghostly and crossed over into one or more societal chords; enabled social and cultural entanglements to strengthen survival mechanism.

4

3

Next course begged attention. Bored she became.

Sub-Set: Sociological Machinations

"What physical attraction means?" Physical attractiveness is degree to which person's physical features are considered aesthetically pleasing or beautiful. Term often implies sexual attractiveness or desirability but can also be distinct from either.

Seductress. Woman who seduces someone, especially one who entices a man into sexual activity. Synonyms. Sounds like a spice, she thought. Temptress, siren, femme fatale, enchantress, sorceress, Delilah, Circe, Lorelei, Mata Hari; flirt, coquette, Lolita; vamp, hoochie, witch; tart; loose woman; fizgig, wanton, strumpet.

What is seductive look? Seductive describes fascinating magnetic pull that someone or something has, an attractive quality that tempts you in some way. Seductive person catches your eye and won't let it go.

How can I look sexually attractive? Here are seven simple things you can do that instantly make you more attractive. Be altruistic. Use metaphorical compliments. Look directly at someone and smile. Wear red. Modify your walk. Nod your head. Adopt an expansive posture. She stood and moved over to wall mirror. Looked herself up and down and sideways and backwards. "Expansive yes."

How can I look hot and attractive? So, in spirit of feeling our most awesome, here are eight things you can do to look more attractive, backed by science. Keep Your Teeth White. Go for Voluminous Hair Style. Take Care of Your Skin. Have Red Lipstick Handy. Searched lipstick.

"Eww yuck," entered her mind. Not sure why. And Put on That Red Dress. Red? What is Red? Will get back to it later. Mimic. Accentuate Your Symmetry. She stood. Jiggled her body elements.

Moved around room in random jiggle mode. "Not bad." Be Confident. Floor looked cleaner, anyway.

How do you flirt? Flirting In-Person. Make eye contact. Eye contact is best and easiest thing you can do to start flirting. Smile. Start talking. Initiate a conversation. Keep it light. "Oh, no, not light," she mused. "Oh, wait, that light." Use body language to communicate your intentions. Break touch barrier. Compliment other person early in conversation.

What is flirtatious behavior? Spouses are often sexually interested in other people but are so uncomfortable with idea that they repress their sexual feelings. Their true feelings, however, come across through their behavior—acting overly friendly, interested, engaged, and so on. Unconscious flirtatious behavior. She looked up "Spouses". More Search Machine grinding ensued. "Ancient construct," she read. Guessed, she did, that appearances matter in some social constructs.

What facial features make women attractive? Facial symmetry has been shown to be considered attractive in women, and men have been found to prefer full lips, high forehead, broad face, small chin, small nose, short and narrow jaw, high cheekbones, clear and smooth skin, and wide-set eyes. "Mirror, mirror, on wall, display my buttocks, moles and all." She laughed at herself, but Search Machine responded and then projected glow view before her eyes.

"Not bad. Not bad at all," she critiqued at herself. Yet to become convinced of such advice, she resolved to use her buttocks sparingly, and only in an emergency. She looked at it again. Adjusted four of her arm tentacles into grip vice fashion and squeezed each of two cheeks. She rubbed them all around; then jiggled each; then bent over for varied structural changes observation; then patted, then patted harder. Strange stimulations attacked parts of her body. "Enough of that, now," she entreated. She couldn't wait for this Mission to start, much less end. Search Machine obliged and clicked off glow view. Dusty light rays sprayed into tiny balls and disappeared.

What is most attractive eye color? Green eyes most attractive eye color. Green: 20.3%. Light blue:

16.9%. Hazel: 16.0%. Dark blue: 15.2%. Gray: 10.9%. Honey: 7.9%. Amethyst: 6.9%. Brown: 5.9%.

What males find sexy? "Ugh. One of those worlds." She became mystified about how she might fit into such box. Simple ways to get him to notice you. Smile. Today. Do not hide in corner. Stay away from hiding yourself in corner, with furniture or plants. Ask for his help. Talk about your hobbies. Do not dress for your girlfriends. Look him in eye. Avoid obvious. Go out alone or with one other friend. She looked up friend. "Oh." She tried to remember, "practice friend persona".

How can females be interesting? An error has occurred. Reboot in progress ... . She waited for female construct to load. "Here it is." Develop new skills. Ensure that other people find you interesting by making yourself helpful in any situation. Be curious. Learn how to tell good story. Have three good stories ready to share. Listen and show compassion. Ask good questions. Say what you think. Follow your interests.

She became confused about differences between actions of males and females and why they mattered to specific biological elements of being. She tapped in more search words, but no enlightenment presented itself except connection between female and woman and male and man. "Stupid," she thought. Need for sexual attractions devices and elements of existence seemed irrelevant but apparently necessary knowledge in dimensional world target destination. "More complicated than I guessed."

How can I be more romantic? Confused she was. She already knew Roman was Old Earth civilization; dead one in long ago extinct humanoid Dimension world she learned about when much younger, during study of ancient extinct cultures, even before her Training regimen began. She knew tic was sound wave, time moment noise. How these words formed together into meaning rather confounded her.

Search: Romantic Meaning

Result: Conducive to or characterized by expression of love.

She started to grasp it, in meaning, factually, but only ephemerally. Socialization involved emotional dances accentuated by physical movements.

She loved to dance. Helped clean her environment. Did not realize it helped clean mind, perhaps soul, too. "To love dance is to love mind and soul." She thought about that thought concept for bits. How to translate into connections among another or other beings still concerned her. "Nuances needed." Put that search on hold for another Training session. Skip. But system would not let her skip.

10 Super Easy Ways to Be More Romantic. Wax nostalgic. Ninety-eight percent of romance is remembering not to take each other for granted. Do not overshare. There's fine line between intimacy and TMI. Searched "TMI".

Result: Too Much Information.

She guessed secrecy somewhat important. Mask, to hide behind. Never give up too much. Little is more than enough. Emotional indigestion gurgled in her bowels. She laughed. Go on dates. Exchange just-because gifts or treats. Nonsensical acts important, she mentally noted. Got it. Engage in random PDA. "Huh? What does tech system device have to do with it?" She entered search mode again.

Search: Cross-ref PDA meaning

Noun. "Noun? Who fracking entered this data?" Already not liking this target destination. Pace yourself, she reminded. We can do this. She tried to convince her dual-sided brains of matters at hand. Noun. Palmtop computer that functions as personal organizer but also provides email and Internet access. "That can't be correct," she thought. Why would tech tools become important for personal relationships of beings? She wanted to check other tools used in personal relationships, but short time begged move on.

Sub-Set Recheck: Cross-ref PDA meaning

What is PDA sexually? PDA stands for public displays of affection. They are gestures of physical intimacy that occur around others. Physical intimacy is method of demonstrating one's feelings through touch. PDA can exist in variety of relationships, be it platonic, romantic, or sexual. Write love notes. Brag about your partner in public. Compliment your partner.

"Ugh." She began to wonder about sanity of Old Earth humanoids. She never even modified Search parameters for "sexually" Sub-Set. Still, many Dimension worlds were modeled after such civilization entities. Results continued Search System drips.

What is most attractive height for a girl? Women tended

to want to be two inches taller than average, while men tend to want to be one inch taller. In most cases – except for men under 5'8" and women under 5'4" – majority of people in given 4-inch height range picked height within their own range as personal "ideal".

What is considered cheating in marriage?
Search: Cross-ref Marriage meaning
Noun

1. legally or formally recognized union of two people as partners in personal relationship (historically and in some jurisdictions specifically union between man and woman).
2. combination or mixture of two or more elements.

Strange. Marriage? Why? Separate gender designations? She did not understand purpose or reason or cause for such unions or biological designations.

Resources efficiency? Do shared materials begin acculturation connection point? Socialization hygiene issues confounded her ability to understand such arrangements.

Why would hoarding supply become necessary? Search Machine System gurgled up more info. Sub-Set: Infidelity meaning.

Synonyms include cheating, straying, adultery (when married), being unfaithful, or having an affair constituted violation of couple's assumed or stated contract regarding emotional and/or sexual exclusivity. More results and potential inquiries vomited forth.

Is infidelity Hereditary? Is Infidelity Genetic? Genes associated with sensation-seeking behaviors, such as drinking alcohol or gambling, may also be associated with sexual promiscuity and infidelity. Findings suggest genetic variation may indeed influence sexual behavior.

Is infidelity common? In general, men are more likely than women to cheat: 20% of men and 13% of women reported they've had sex with someone other than their spouse while married, according to data. Infidelity for both men and women increased during middle ages. Old Earth history, primary source, but other Dimensional entities engineered similar concepts of two person or more unions, either formal or informal, perhaps to ensure species survival. "Infidelity increased due to plagues and diseases killing off society?" She wondered.

How many types of cheating are there? While definitions vary couple-to-couple, there are some common underlying factors, such as secrecy, deception, and emotional volatility. Five definitive types of cheating and surprisingly, two of them may not even involve your partner. Ariadne wondered. She kept seeing references to men and women. "Women? Do they mean females? Opposite gender?" She wondered what attraction to opposites purposed. Checked on words again. Understood.

What percentage of marriages survive infidelity? Percentage of marriages where one or both spouses admit to infidelity, either physical or emotional, is 41 percent. 60 percent of men and 40 percent of women will have an affair at some point in their marriage. "Marriage is so outdated," she groaned.

For feelings of wide range of love interpretation emotions, she was recommended songs. "Songs?"

She wondered where Chants were. Old Earth history blurts sprayed into multiple glow screens before her vision, one screen for each song. Her eyes bobbed back forth and up down to swim amidst it all. She would check again later, but allowed song sounds to download into her emotion-side brain. "Odd Old Earth humanoids. Odd."

Search Songs:

Source: ____________________

More Search Machine dribbles.

Source: Old Earth Music

See Diana Ross, Mahogany

See Peter Frampton, I'm In You

See Led Zeppelin, Whole Lotta Love

See Albinoni, Adagio in G Minor

See Skylark, Wildflower

See Pachelbel, Canon In D

"Can't be right," she imagined. Such music identified Old Earth sounds only. Was Old Earth some base point for all evolved species? Perhaps Universe used it as experiment for construction of other planetary cultures? She wanted to search other world or Dimension databases but Research time winded down quick. Six ancient world tunes seemed enough to consider. Enough for starters. Maybe get to others later.

She listened. Her mind tingled. Her body sparked in varied places. "Unsettling." She tried to tamp down varied parts of each brain compartment and allowed emoted sparks to leak from her consciousness, yet she saved musical sounds and words for later reference in analytical block compartment. "Don't need all this cully swoggle now."

But Wildflower intrigued. She requested additional information.

Wildflower. Flower of uncultivated variety or flower growing feely without human intervention. She searched database further. Any flowering plant not genetically manipulated. Plants growing without intentional humanoid aid, particularly those flowering in spring and summer in woodlands, prairies, and mountains.

Seasons? Seasoning? Were songs emotion emitters or food enhancers? Wildflowers were source of all cultivated garden varieties of flowers. Searched further, she did.

Accentuate system data. Incorporate wildflower entity into consciousness ... amidst scent glands.

See further search data related to wildflowers. Old Earth database entry: What do different flowers symbolize? Each flower has color, fragrance, and personality of its own. Red roses symbolize love and whites symbolize innocence. Different flowers symbolize different emotions. Lotus flower symbolizes rebirth. Wild parsnip plant (Pastinaca sativa).

See unknown Old Earth source. She requested more information. Woman jogging had slid into bush on roadside, she stood up, brushed herself and went home. Days later she would pay for this with excruciating pain and second-degree burns.

Murphy (her name) had stumbled into wild parsnip plant (Pastinaca sativa). Such weed, also known as poison parsnip and hobo parsnip, is wild version of root vegetable that resembles carrot. Carrot glow box hovered before her vision. But while cream-colored roots are edible, plant's sap is treacherous.

Just like hogweed, another similar looking weed found on side of road, wild parsnip sap contains furanocoumarins, which are compounds that cause severe burns. Sap is toxic and basically strips body's ability to control UV radiations from sunlight. Basically, sunlight activates compounds in oil and leads to what is essentially extreme sunburn, which can worsen with moisture and heat. She ended Old Earth database search.

5

4

Her wonder time started. In this Dimension was there disease of nighttime which caused daytime dwellers to become evil? Was disease spread by wildflowers?

Search: Humanoid

Range Narrow: Demon

Sub-Set: Nazran

More Specific: Assassin

Name: Ariadne

Wildflower: creature or sentient being that travels to many different places and can flourish anywhere. It can become invisible to tech photo devices. It kills by smothering victim, only before noon.

Search: Noon

Per Old Earth database, morning started at 12:01AM, ended at Noon, so sometimes work progressed in darkness, when no birds sang but slept, then presaged dawn birds' symphony.

Okay. Apparently Mission Target world is similar to Old Earth habitat. 24-hour daily cycle.

Additional Relevant Data: Sapiosexual, person who is attracted to intelligent people

Sometimes ghost voices called to her, from Search Engine internal machinations, usually to direct her onto Target path, sometimes to misdirect. Voices were not fully explained, left mystery of whether she was humanoid, god, spirit, or demon, or combinations thereof.

"There's no humanoid worth dying for. None." Her thought. Not sure why such thought voice infected her, almost involuntarily, in this moment. She could not let it out verbally. Thoughts could be considered treasonous, and were monitored, but still considered somewhat involuntary and thus, less harmful to her planetoid organization structure. Would make her seem weak, though. Selfish. She had all she could do to prevent room monitors imbedded in walls and ceiling from picking up her thought vibrations in too high raised wave level.

She strived for skills that could defeat any rational purpose of living beings with just strands of her hair. She allowed her dark and thin hair strands to extend at will until each pointed outward in circular fashion from each hair follicle near one meter in length until it became sharp as dagger tips. It is okay to exploit weaknesses. But she wondered of death; scene; like Acts in Theatre Play; dramatic. Final curtain.

Humanoid descriptions of varied cultures disturbed her

emotions. Pretext. Moment of. Postscript. Not much data

available in Search System for such topic rumination. Scrubbed by her Superiors from Training Manual? She knew work arounds.

Her tech skills not completely tapped or explored by her mentors, nor encouraged. She kept unknowns hidden. Developed on her own. Road she forged and travelled to stir wild free will. Pretend to need them, Controller and Ordinator alike, in some circumstances. Probe their weaknesses purpose served her curiosities. Edible intellectual treasures. Almost to a whisper tone, she thoughted. Her hand slipped. Data generation scrambled. Roulette wheel spin. "Why did 'roulette' word pop mind?"

Subject: War Games

Sub-Set: Individual Survival Defense Tactics

"Don't think I need this data," she thought. Worth look for future assignments. Getting ahead of herself, she realized. Why not. Ahead of Data Read Assimilation schedule anyway. She realized even her thoughts could activate Search Engine tech. And so, Training continued.

Enactment: Strategy

List forming. Room silence tucked her into calmness envelope. Results.

Overwhelming odds. Rebel odds. Top down decimation tactics. Day compared to night strengths and weaknesses. She thought perhaps useful in tiny societal situations. Connected, she did, to her Target's strategy. Data push screamed at her. Mind pain, on both sides of head. Headache echoed badly, temporarily blinded her inside and out. Consciousness faded, faded, darkness covered her mind in syrupy layers. Slowly receded. Thought horizon formed, receded, reformed. System resistance to data formation apparent.

Used her mind, she did, to encourage data collaboration unto conclusion resulted. Bock in System. She inserted her right brain energy to solve riddle of diversion. Interruption intentional, she surmised. System anticipated user curiosity and tried block of knowledge.

Anger from left brain ignited. To keep knowledge from her she deduced as system wildness. "Programmed into search profile," she thought. "Why don't they want me to know this material?" Wildflower pollen, System seemed to generate.

She needed rest now. Set, she did, Training System to slowly stream into her brains necessary background Research Data about her Targets. She reclined upon rest mat, all white in color, in humanoid form to allow body adaptation. Set Data Continue Load during somber somnambulance state; incorporated into her brains knowledge about how to identify Target victims. Data loaded from local police precincts of each Target's Dimension home world. She checked files, computer data.

Training System had automatically loaded Time Bend cycle, so entry and exit of data happened in between Time folds. Caused less curiosity for relevant police authorities. Also protected her against schemes of Target worlds to undermine her Button Hand duties or discover her identity.

Humanoids and all living things appeared as statue-like objects around her during this phase. As distraction for potential local authority discovery of her machinations, she mentally enjoyed honbap dining. In such manner, her alone status would serve as screen or curtain to avoid detection. Chance for some peace. Solitude among horde. Look at me; last thing you will see.

Once Target victims identified, she studied them, their patterns, aromas, usually instigated an accidental meeting. Learned to know each Target entity; some were sex predators, so she practiced luring them into their own death, one marked by their exact sexual preferences and madness, which she imposed on them. The Simulations used real data, but her activities were exercised as Training practice. She could not harm them now, or execute the Sentencing orders, only practice how to do so.

One Target was mongrel child, or young teenager, who had created havoc wherever he arrived, injuring people and other children, killing animals for sadistic sport, learning. Her dealings with him were more passive, as his actions upon others bounced back to his own self, injuring him also. She convinced him, passively, he couldn't die, so he perpetrated something stupid, and killed himself in the process.

Two were young adult women, Hugwanes, best friends, who had cheated and schemed to enrich themselves and left many victims behind. She determined their weakness to be cancer. She laid tentacles on them to accelerate spread of it. Watched them slowly die, miserably, off and on, as they came into flower shop she occupied for Mission cover.

These Hugwanes entered to celebrate conquests of their victims. Each time they bought flowers she made sure to touch them or touch objects she anticipated they would touch while looking around as she sold good luck charms type trinkets. Essentially, they were unknowingly yet gleefully killing themselves further every time they touched objects.

One was Corpolvander banker/stockbroker, mind developed essence of evil, serial killer, theft of client funds, adulterous relationships, she contemplated killing him herself to end misery of those he tortured. She came across this man during course of Mission, he wasn't on Mission Target list. She could no longer tolerate his mayhem evil imposed upon Target Dimension planetoid prison colony. She wondered if he was humanoid from another Dimension, sent to assassinate Marks designated for him by his Societal structure. Perhaps he was just like her. She wasn't sure at this time.

Ariadne power source flowed from flowering plants for this Mission, as they were convenient and available source of energy at Mission Target location. By necessity, her punishments must come near fields, flower shops, depending on locale. By selling flowers and plants to potential targets, she reeled them into her emotional killing lair.

To seek perfection was fool's errand. She realized this thought as distraction from her Research; also sign of possible brain drain. Too much time lost, wasted on laments. She wondered how she got assigned to this place. "Why" stuck her side like pins, needles. Unidentified source voices swirled like windstorm in analytical brain.

"Do you need gods?"

"Sure. You got one?"

"Any openings?"

"Quite many. Are you god?"

"No."

"Well, then. Nothing else to say."

"What if I was god?"

"Yes or no."

"Yes."

"Yes, what?"

"Yes. I will take job. When do I start?"

"10,000 years ago. Now find new ways to F things up, will you?"

"Quiet. Riot. Calm. Crazy. Subliminal. Spacey."

"What?"

"Your design. Environment. Universe, as it were."

"Little of each, I suppose."

"Smorgasbord. Got it."

"Being fodder."

"Illuminate, please."

"Lower level entities in need of domination,

direction, stimulation. In other words, your subjects."

"Never thought about it."

"Done."

"Wait one minute. I didn't choose."

"Yes. You did."

"What? How?"

"Done again."

"Come on, now."

"Can't. Lots of gods waiting for assignment."

"Geesh."

"Next!"

Dialogue screen confused her. Voices unrecognized, location not clear. "Eating alone," she thought. "Must be voices beyond curtain, or her actual reclined state nearby in Training facility."

She wondered if Ventnoirs had infiltrated some of the police locations. Time Bend's didn't always stop them, given their abilities to consume brains to extract information for profit. Time Bend status allowed presence in multiple locations at same time. She had become concerned whether Data Loading Cycle neared an end.

Still masked, she was, behind Time Bend curtain. Still

reclined on rest mat at Training facility. Needed to collect her essence into one Entity, back at Training facility.

Assignment data transplanted ethereally into her twin brains. Absorption started. "An adults only dark fantasy of inter-dimensional origin. Many dimensional inhabitant locations are familiar of predators' needs. Button Hand demon's wisdom and wares were required to restore serenity, for as little time as it would last, even one changed moment meant lots in sheepfolds of chaos." Distinct thought occurred to her.

"Going to need blackout curtains." Too much daytime light on her face, outer skin, would sap her strength. Ventnoirs would scheme to steal anyone's brain, for high enough price. Button Hand knowledge could be worth fortunes. Goth designed clothes, her determined preference for Missions, would help greatly to deflect light.

Rest over. Safe at Training Facility quarters. Time Bend session completed.

6

5

She checked for weapons needs targeted to specific Mission objectives and assigned Targets.

Weapons Cache: Attack Deflection

Purpose: Exogenous Defense

Mission Target Class: Infinite Life Entity

Result: Shock Suit

"Better bring Shock Suit," she thought. "Suit exterior temporarily stuns anyone or anything that it comes in contact with." Suit range detected ambient vibrations from things like wind, rivers, ocean waves and human activities. Would buy her precious time in difficult situation, especially during violent encounters. She sensed potential "hinky nature" about some Targets. Shaped Suit to her form and then designed optics to help attract or detract attention, as necessary. Strange magic, it was. Another prompt appeared on screen.

Result Supplementary: Collection Shroud

"Good idea. Clean up detritus mess for later analysis, specimen procurement, disposal of unnecessary parts, and

available edibility usage." Her anatomy could handle any of these needs, including temporary storage.

Searched her mind she did to attract other Mission needs, but just empty spaces echoed there for bit of time. Forgotten forbidden. Nugget thoughts chunked against her psyche. Splattered, they did, into tiny specs, flakes uneven. Forbidden forgotten. Curious. Must look up, research, such mangled stone wall batters. No time now. Nonsense, anyway. Comfortable numbness resulted deep down inside her in places somewhere lost. Darkness invaded in irregular patterns unavoidable.

She was not afraid of dark. She had long ago combatted such wretched sentience smothers. They now served her as blanket to warm her spirit. Too easy to just close her legs together and skull crush. Just and right did not exist, only dark and light. Spirit adapted to essence and essence rewarded effort as water coaxed life. Meddling thought patterns she swatted away. "Dubious is as dubious does."

Budded talents seeded into her being she developed to fuller potential since youngling age. Her Training expanded into humanoid senses recognitions, but some were lost to her, in meaning.

Flexible like octopus. Diet intake like possum, nightly incursions preferred. Bat radar vision. Dark side of moon she desired mostly; slowly; regularly. "Jeez. When do I know enough?" No endpoint to learned skills knowledge and performance. She wondered but only for seconds. Time wasters. Just do. Comes together later. She wanted to masturbate. Too much Training, not enough relaxing. Later. Later. Might as well be forever time. Time. Final crusher of all things, delights, sins, inhibitions, machinations, aspirations.

Some issues: detritus removal. Her ambient anatomy processed consumed food on her world like an amoeba. Not much as it was incorporated into her system and dissolved, but in Mission new world, she must adjust to different form of detritus removal via mouth, liquid extractions, or poop function which irritated hell out of her. At first poop ingestion she realized hated for it. Wanted to plug it and reroute process along internal organs, unchanged in transformation. She encountered sex shop near where she worked at floral shop, explored it and found butt plugs after rather direct inquiry of service person who was not embarrassed at all by question. Its use was explained to her quite readily.

Stuff that dripped from nose also irritated her. Solace escaped her mental grasp too often. Flower allergy unknown.

Provided all knowledge of Target world from microbes to environment, through edible and drinkable avenues and invented use tools. She would encounter nothing, object or entity biological or chemical or ... ? Including sounds, thoughts, feelings, emotions, personality types (highly predictable for sentient species) absent comprehensive knowledge analytics. Never enough to know when relying on Seeker (microscopic scouts and mechanical devices used to map Target world from inside and out) technology, perhaps petty disadvantage, at best. Inoculation against procreation possibility provided during Mission prep for Tasks when such temptations could entrap Targets. Her current Mission required inoculation.

Inoculation. She gathered it meant somewhat exotic world virus critters awaited her incarnation. Drawback. No chemical could transform her mind-set to match interpersonal relationships she would map out in Target world. In this regard, creativity and specific machination plans set her on proper road, yet destination results would be more difficult to achieve. Readiness confidence eluded her analysis. Not good mental signage, she worried.

Procreation activity prohibited. Permission required for species evolution. Accidental procreation terminated potential future Mission Assignments. Us and Them no longer existed in her world. Only Us. Them meant enemy, primarily. Allies only temporary friends. Those were rules of her culture.

Survival first had benefitted such existence long. To live was not about taking away pain; more about gaining experience to manage it; placate demands of it. Absence of pain certified sudden death potential. Sorrows milled. Zeugma's dominated, cursed such culture, perhaps many, perhaps all. Weeping eyes and weeping hearts drained dry. Interchangeable. Demons often scorched such existence parameters. Sorrows flowed unbending in her thoughts. Regulations prohibited surrenders to such madness. Her thoughts meandered into things left unsaid.

Typical demon greeting or goodbye:

"Courtesy."

"And so, you."

"Call role."

Programmed, she was, to think such thoughts and play such organs. Training demons harkened. Names started to bark out from elevated room speakers. She tensed in bits as session neared end. Then, her name blared out from speaker horn. Her own name soothed her in sound during her existence. In this moment, tension strummed her body throughout; audible strains of door hinge swings opened in her mind; reveille called to first Mission. She overheard din of Meeting Hall banter.

"Zeugmas. I'm a GC, Cleaner Level."

"Nothing but Garbage Collector?"

"And yet, this world isn't better place, but for me."

"We shall see, Garbage Collector."

"Only three sentient types in any world. Takers, makers, and fakers."

"Didn't ask for your wisdom."

Ariadne considered herself as worthy as DC. Diamond Cutter. Upon arrival to Meeting Hall, she added further voice to sarcastic shrill din.

"We are all combinations of three, at one time or another. Will determines result."

"You just clear deadwood."

"Justly. Beautifully."

Another Button Hand entered Meeting Hall, voice inflection nervous.

"What? Shut up."

"She tapped listen vein."

"Always in choice, it is. Bless Mother Nature. Curse Father Time. All In buffet table. All vine shines."

"Praying to gods won't help."

"No one, nothing escapes. All that remains is eternal shine."

"Make yourself pretty needed, then get on with it."

She thought, "Great, just more hurry in scurry. Patience is

mystery to Management. Rumination piqued. Destination pends. Splintered paw."

"Predictable."

"Eeegggeee."

"Nasty."

Belch sounds irritated her, yet anatomical relief created sweet calm. Mind full.

"Courtesy."

"And so, you."

Management called halt to excessive banter over loudspeaker. Attention directed to glow screen. Each Button needed to choose one Management gift for use during assigned Mission. Ariadne contemplated gift choice while other made their designation known.

She used scent pheromones to home in on sentient needs of prey. Reason for her knowledge of attractive flower's scents. Attractor. Distractor. Scent became her spider's web. Mission Tasks called to her from deep mind mill. Still, too many things left unsaid, unlearned, unpracticed.

Skills offered. Choose one gift. List review posted. Two

highlighted. Emulation and Temptation.

"Run, rabbit, run," she fooled.

Warning cautions.

"Excessive use of these traits creates need for socialization. Not recommended for alone beings. Fits of anger could expose Mission Tasks detectable by highly sentient beings, negating skill gift effect."

She thought long time. Warning repeated in her head, again and again. Realized, she did, some Missions successful hinged on gift skill granted and otherwise chosen. She did not know what is love. Concern about such emotion caused struggle in her mind. Failure to learn fast enough forged doom path in her mind.

She chose Temptation. Her body, mind, spirit, eyes became temptations themselves if she could master such skills. She pressed adjust for better control. Highest level presented greatest danger to wielder. Longer adaptation time. Mid-range level would give her better time to learn, adapt, practice. No means available to truncate skill development curve. Danger remained.

She reviewed list again. One other Mission skill appeared as bonus choice to complement Temptation. It was Emotion. As skill, it could become important for her to enable entrapment of Targeted Marks. See below recommended. She directed glow screen to provide more info. State of mind ability to affect DNA.

Epigenetics. More data flowed from screen.

"Three different studies, done by different teams of scientists, proved something extraordinary. But when new research connected these three discoveries, something shocking was realized. Something hiding in plain sight. Humanoid emotion literally shaped world around us. Not just our perception of the world, but reality itself.

Humanoid emotion produced effects which defied conventional laws of physics. Removal of DNA from humanoid subject, even placed 50 miles away, had same identical responses in time. Conclusion: donor and DNA can communicate beyond space and time.

Another example: light photons, which make up world around us, were observed inside vacuum. Their natural locations were completely random. Humanoid DNA was then inserted into vacuum. Shockingly, photons were no longer acting random. They precisely followed geometry of DNA. Possibly new field of energy.

Conclusion: humanoid DNA literally shaped behavior of light photons that make up world around us. Stunning realization that if our emotions affect DNA and our DNA shapes world around us, then our emotions physically change world around us. Further, we are connected to our DNA beyond space and time. We create our reality by choosing it with our feelings."

"Well," she thought, "at least they are providing added

skill sets for Mission Task accomplishment, and survival."

Another realization poked at her. She would not encounter only humanoids during her Missions. Other creature encounters Training not provided. Brushed off such thought distractions, for now.

Before rest, she requested summary of Governmental properties for advanced civilizations. Government entities common to sentient being worlds. Entities characterized demonstrate control of education, marketing of goods, entertainment industries, and essential elements of communications and dissemination of knowledge.

She refined search. At this point in time, all other Button Hands had exited Meeting Hall to refine Mission Task Assignment preparations. Search result appeared: Primary Governmental systems in Galactic area.

Totalitarianism. Result. Absolute control by small group of power mongers, either elected or otherwise (violence). Dissent punished, indiscriminately. Some Transgressors eliminated either by death or imprisonment. Societal rules applied to all citizens except small in-control power groupings.

Democracy. Result. Control of all aspects of humanoid interaction. Dissent somewhat tolerated but punished by government regulation; media destruction of citizen reputations to create alienation and emotional, societal imprisonment away from general populace. Most rules apply to societal group. Most rules not enforced against governmental Controllers.

Communism. Result. Control of all aspects of humanoid interaction, primarily assured through assured destruction of dissenters and dissent movements as needed. Rules malleable at discretion of Officials in power.

Fascism. Result. See Communism.

Republic. Result. No findings.

She was confused. No expressions of Republic meaning available, as if topic details erased from system. She rebooted system to return at this knowledge point. Too tired to wait for results. Rest begged her attention. Perhaps Republic data not deemed necessary Training knowledge for Mission goals; or perhaps considered subversive. Too tired to resist further obstruction of knowledge tricks seemingly bugged into System Training. She yearned, too, for more coverage of sensation senses in more detail.

"Tech them," she cursed. Probably not first Button Hand to express venial emotions in Training sessions, she guessed. Won't be last, she thought.

Rest thoughts won out. She exited Meeting Hall, but door hinges cringed against closure. "GC could handle door hinge issues," she presumed. Plenty of time for her two brains and three hearts to absorb powers of these new skills during trip to Target Dimension.

Upon return to her housing cubicle, she set Training System to bleed further needed knowledge into her brains via micro-patch during Mission destination trip. Pre-set sentient brain interaction with patch to occur on as needed basis. Analytical enlightenment solutions hopefully would rise to top at appropriate moment situations. It was times like these, wondered she, whether Training, or merely, Programming resulted. Both? Time to go.

Mission Status: Readied.

Training Status: Completed.

7

6

"Enter mission chamber."

She obliged, after deep breath movements. Chamber reduced size. Her only comfort form required rolling up into sphere size, truncating her movement along chilled containment system sides. Thought popped into her head.

"If you allow yourself to be ruled by idiots, best result available is to evolve into an idiot." Alternatives, banned.

Her outside Training Program source search involuntarily progressed. She became scared. Thought bombs should not gain entrance into her sentient mind unless she activated process voluntarily. Then, she realized, her current process would result in subconscious mind state.

She understood and pre-set one brain function to record sub-conscious thoughts during mission travel time. Still, not sure why subliminal thoughts started invasion. Like footprints in sand or hand-prints on dusty walls, sub-conscious furious prodded her along. At conclusion of entry into site location, she tapped telepathic brain waves to check her humanoid transformation. She appeared as rolled-up humanoid ball, at pre-birth stage rested in large and long field of varied plants and flowers.

Her origin anatomy included three legs. She now possessed only two. Her six tentacles which extended from waist, sides and back had become two humanoid arms, one flowing downward at each side of rectangular body shape. She struggled to accommodate her organs amidst this truncated form as her natural body structure accommodated a few more feet in height and breadth.

She commenced body attribute functions. Oozed scents from skin pores. Movement of her humanoid appendages, usually hand or foot, close enough to subject, could produce pheromones to intoxicate essence of humanoids or creatures, at which time they should become extremely receptive to suggestion. It was not trick of magic or mystic origin. It was biology, of her Dimensional world. She lamented stringy hair growth. Work on it, she would.

Many creatures in her home world had same capacity, usually stimulated by fear threat or extinctual actions like procreation. Beings on her planet had more intense degree of these biological elements, such that an effect could be created to ensnare prey long enough for kill thrust or otherwise physical incapacitating blow.

Energy concentrations governed by demon's directed sentience skills could turn fist into brick or ballpeen hammer in strength of contour. Sometimes scent barrage incapacitated Target subject enough. Weaker beings were drowned in it, unable to breath unless birthed of gill structure, unable to function, yet still subject to pain transmitters of victim's body. Starvation could result, or catastrophic clumsiness, or general vital organ shutdown of critical anatomy.

Then she realized biological sustenance was not listed on survival list. Why? What if no flowers, trees, seeds of plant life existed in realm destination? Perhaps not information needed for Mission Tasks? Or maybe Training poke nuance she critically ignored as means to finish Instruction segments quicker? Second guessing; third guessing; fourth guessing. Point missed, she thought, uneasily.

Must be more like this one, she thought. Otherwise, no food source existed for bug and insect snacks. Wasting energy on wishes and wants, she thought. Conserve it for needs. Perhaps segregation of Target from nutrition sustenance needs was Mission strategy technique ignored by Training System? She pocketed such thoughts for potential future rumination.

Pod Transport shell cleared atmosphere and touched ground in flower field. Her automated senses scanned terrain. Planet and neighborhood location not relevant, except to say it resembled period of life in ancient extinct Old Earth's Baltimore, place where Demons temporarily resided. Helped to learn needs, wants and elegant desires of humanoid species at such location since closely it resembled planetary system in Mission Target Dimension.

Names tempted attachments; became entrap-ments. Purge

her mind, she must, of Mission fears. Constant battle. Safety tugs, perhaps. Anxiety thick flowed through her veins at thoughts of potential dangers. Control them, she must.

Mission Brief circled her mind. What strange world destination Dimension seemed. Beings tor-tured by emotions, and sexual taunts, and ten-sions, yet fighting worst inclinations every turn of geographical clock. No sense in such places. No rest. No seminal belief system. She wondered how her duty would be classified. Avenger. Punisher. Revenger. Enforcer. All bought and paid for, if not for justice, for order. "Who's order?" She wondered. Service provided by her world could be purchased, no questions asked. "Irrelevant," she told herself.

Cursed by treasure of creativity and creative-ness, usage of which resulted in breaks of all tools acquired, and sometimes, in breaks of all coher-ent moments. Puzzles broken. Pieces unfit. Sense, emotion, rationality in progress; essentially creative work served to avoid reality prison walls.

Reality lonely place. Lonely place real. Random. Of all possible addictions, her instructors weighted heed laid heavy on love. Love's tug clouded humanoid thoughts, goals, ambition. Truncated skill growth resulted. Killed growth thoughts. Tainted all being. An evil creation of mind in many Dimensions and worlds of Dimensions. Dimension beings, as their own sole place, once attached to love, suffered great brain fogs inescapable dangerous. Puzzles of no connected pieces stared coldly back into her brains.

"Android Assassin could have been sent for this Mission," she mused. "Emotional skills and choices must be needed", she surmised. Braced against embracement of stem intricacies, she became. Must be part of her learning curve. Big picture pretty. Details just dots, lines, random swishes of brush tools. She worried about details and observations presented to her mind through Training. Accurate? Nuanced? How to decide most relevant senses needed at apt and correct time? Training module for enlightenment, she searched. None found. Glad she chose creativity element for perception mechanism skill.

Day cycles paid no mind to life or death events. Some humanoids and creatures exhibited stronger, more viral and dangerous skill qualities in light. Some assimilated superior qualities amid darkness. She could not assume entities encountered during either cycle status solely occupied each carnivorous carnival event. Murderers, either of quiet passion instigation or maniacal energy bursts created same results. Extinguishment. Elimination. Death.

Upon entry into marked Dimension world, she noticed sounds not encountered in Training regimen. One sound plucked interest. It was steady, regular, grated on her soul at first, like ricket chirps, then blended into vibration scenery as soft auditory accompaniment. Perhaps she should not have nodded off in echomimetic Training sessions. She concentrated to ignore it and succeeded, except for one thought which escaped back into her mind.

"Friendship isn't a suicide pact." She wondered what was "friendship". Such thought not natural or ordinary in Training sessions. Perhaps system bug laying eggs and she was finding them.

"Neighbor" word dangled in screen and blinked on and off. She questioned, "What is neighbor?"

She read meaning data. Realized she needed to practice neighboring. Neighbors neighboring could become important, she thought, to develop connection to Target Marks.

Ricket chirps returned. She interpreted such sounds as warning signals, perhaps beacons of Target Marks' spatial presence. "Anton." When she mentally followed chirps, focused them, narrowed they did into origin point Anton. Thoughts of him, his skills, and devious horrible actions tapped methodically into each of her brains. In each, his Assignment bio migrated near chirps' origin point.

She reviewed analytical brain for recap of Anton's known history. Full well she knew history may be incomplete, depended on factual and researched data usually infected by observer bias. Anton's seminal beef displayed. First and only wife bilked him out of all his money while at same time cheating on him with numerous men and women of varied biological orientation. Some of her paramours, whom he thought were his friends, including his own brother, had become seduced by her charms. He killed all of them and thus began his serial killer career, commenced first motivated by revenge, later by monetary profit motives. Perhaps he learned to enjoy too much his works as profession; or perhaps enjoyed as hobby.

Revenge. He violently freed his psyche from events which caused his suffering, then found he needed further revenge against other women and men and such entities like those of his spouse and her lovers. Profit. He became cruel faker taker. If there existed some reward in extinction of his personal Mission Targets, then once permanently extinguished they became, his faker taker characteristics served as spice. She researched these descriptions of Anton's motivation moments in attempt to further understand or trip up some meaningful purpose. Confounded, she escaped to another research topic.

Her moments of ease were rare. She found way to capture some. Aves creatures, those of feathers and toothless beaked jaws, and there were many in this Dimension world, tweeted musically just before sunrise, perhaps as beacon of hope and harbinger of songs. Although moments twee remained brief, given her anatomical constraints, they had become cherished to her soul rejuvenations, stimulations for her duality brains along synapses of multiple veins. Still, she worried her own aroma, at various times of day, particularly after eating and while digesting edibles, could blow her cover persona.

"I need to find means of excretion detritus concealment."

Again, her brains became infected by worrisome thoughts of most dangerous unofficial Mission Target, Anton. Unofficial in sense he could alter Mission goals. Mission plan required relationships development of some breadth, however incidental, with each of them. As sexual tension manufactured itself in her, she became amorphous in sexuality, but through observation and Training had learned means of temptation and attraction, which allowed her to master any physical parameters necessary to mimic persona bi-sexual, trans-sexual, hetero-sexual, homosexual, or otherwise along spectrum of sensual enticement. Singular sensual pleasure.

There evolved emotion pill for that. In this world, emotional courtship emulated ancient religious rituals in scope, either humanoid or lesser creatures species origin.

Conclusion occurred to her. Male serial killer

Anton's actions emulated those of Watchers descended from her Demon World. He morphed into impossible to kill. She could only imprison him, after he received tastes of his own medicine. Pain of his each kill she observed in Mission records. She replayed his accomplishments in imagination frames. Further Anton data screens, she requested.

He called himself Anton Firenza, worked as real estate agent and dwelling remodeler. He bought foreclosed upon properties cheap, then after renovation he would resell them for profit. But in process of renovations he had created traps in home for his victims to be caught into, then he tortured and killed them, then disposed of them. Ugly business it was. Films of his deeds he kept as souvenirs.

He only owned modest number of homes in varied neighborhoods, but buyers would disappear or skip out, at wretched hands of Anton, then home would go up for auction and he would rebuy it cheap, fix it up again, and start process all over again. Some of his fortune started when as gopher for real estate company, he invented machine that sucked up dust. He would take his invention to homes and clean them up. He would plug in vacuum type machine which had blower to irritate and disperse dust and dirt into room air, then series of long extended hoses would suck in air particles in few minutes, sucking air dry of dust and particles. All he had to do was run it in room and it would clean and clear in few minutes.

What sound disturbed her air, and why there it existed? Many times, too many, not enough, and many more, she wondered about her Mission. These moments inside and shortened time events brought skunk dread aroma of emotions to collective mind forefront.

Anton studied chemistry in college, with purpose specific, it seemed, to explore dark arts of humanoid manipulation. His lust for life scenes ended in death moments, for his victims. Stimulated him incredibly. His personal notes even indicated imagination of how death would become him. Those moments read more horrible. Ariadne was uncertain how this pandemic personality flaw originated in Anton. Exploit it she must or fail miserably, interminably.

Chemistry he engorged upon, essentially for greedy, lustful, shameless purpose. He learned to lust for death not of himself but for his victims. Perhaps both, Ariadne wondered. Victims Anton studied meticulously and at length, looking for their strengths, weaknesses, vulnerabilities. Moments to exploit them, he sought. Ariadne looked for flaws in Anton's personality. Anton's personality. Weapon unto itself.

Her Training sessions assessed designated need skills of deception. Use of mirrors, glass, reflective materials such as Arcade games glass to judge effect of her pheromone transfers. Her pheromones were so strong she sometimes attracted varied animals like dog, cat, squirrel, racoon, rat, and insects like bee, praying mantis, spider, roach. Some of these are food for her. Protein. Her biologic system digested almost anything of protein or carbohydrate content, much like snakes. Her preternatural changeling skills allowed for acclimation to camouflage amidst environmental surroundings.

For instance, conformity meant to become invisible in

billion waves sea. She confirmed her dress style to blend in. Dark cape from just below knee joints flowed upwards into loose cranium hood wrap; shredded, cuffed tight pants, dark in color tone; black running shoes. Although she did not need to utilize undergarments, given her skin tenuity, she learned during Mission Research such wardrobe accessories served as bait for some Targets.

Seduction Queue: Suggestions

Ariadne Mission Persona: Characteristics

Delivery Method: Auditory

Diminutive in spirit and appearance, smallish, permitted for predator seduction as they looked for easy prey. Some Marks demonstrated ability of communal adaption to surroundings. Others were able to modulate surroundings into designs which served their needs. Each such ability granted access to food sources, comfort zone protections, and accentuation of attack or defense mechanisms. She targeted best and most effective temptation and curiosity social ingredients. Examples commenced, orally, as she tired of eyeballs' usage accumulation strain.

"Her toenails were so long she could tap out Gregorian Chant on floor tiles."

"Cursed by thought; worse by thoughts; tangled in pin prick sowings of ruminated entanglements; always, always cloth became shroud."

"Perhaps evil behind smile created cruelest cut."

"Morning betrayed slow death of darkness. Evening restored curtain birth of light. Just opposite in Demon World. Light knifed as sting no less sharp. Her joy in this world involved sensuous bath in full moons' light; Lunar shine luxury in her world."

She greatly enjoyed sound and tonality of base Tech Log voice. Helped her acquire personality for Target world domain.

"Watch out for sin stealers. They take money from clients for self-flagellation after absorbing sin and hide it mongo among dark places of Black Cloud Dimension."

She began to more firmly realize, in her Demon world, there was never mental peace. Always there remained another entity, dual personality, roaming among her brains. Characteristic of such world. She surrendered to same countenance level. Randomly assigned thoughts to another, for analytical practice. Simple network of surveillance to better control insatiable complexities of sideways Demon existence. Always something to bump into, shoebox style. Still free to find another one, shoebox, to rant and roam and storm and groan. Echoes talked back, and voices crashed like ocean waves, or soothed as such upon mind skin, depending on harbinger of strain.

"Absolute zero. Kelvin Negative 459." Book reference.

Sound of Tech system voice startled her. She forgot to

disconnect voice prompt mode. Anyway, she had read that book during her Demon world youth time. Tech voice popped digital picture in front of Ariadne's eyes. She always liked that cover.

To escape miasma of her drizzled mind ramblings, she blurted out word "Food". Hungry she was. Tech voice intoned.

"Food. How an entity eats directly correlates to cultural origin charms. Ariadne should never eat or imbibe in public. Presence purpose potentially becomes exposed."

Wince face scrunched Ariadne's cheeks. Roaches, rats for snacks, yet they were similar into appearance of torks and ferts. Close friends torks and ferts had become to her in her world, so she knew she would have to resist temptation to communicate with them on Target planet. Out of such habit she must rip from. Explained to herself needs.

She could never publicly starve for sustenance or Mission goals would be compromised, yet blood tempted as sweet wine. "Do not eat torks. Do not eat ferts." At least, publicly, she reminded herself. She programmed such thoughts into her analytical brain, then allowed it to reconfigure emotion brain side. Allayed restaurant visits urge, she trusted. Later, she would lash her brains during free thoughts time. "I hope to remember my own counseling advice."

Some rules. Follow instructions. If torment of subject Target required during task, then dispense and conclude. Torment Task not usually ordered in newbie ranks due to complicated nature of set-up stage. If instructions not properly followed, Button Hand recall resulted. Then intricate retraining required which involved infliction Tasks of living as victim Target for punishment, and to serve further as insight revelation. Avoided repeating errors in future Missions, if granted such honor.

After each Mission Task completion, final remembrance ceremony remained important, for Ariadne determined which bodies and souls would become sewn into ground amidst life resurrection or life extermination elements. Purpose designed to prevent undesirable spread of genetic elements else they regenerated and multiplied into chaos.

Ceremony involved. Words, prayer-like; respect for each soul regardless of her sentiment; strictly fitted into Mission purpose of Entity World or Dimension which hired and paid for Button Hand services.

Victim study. Her key skill resided in sniffing out her prey. Aroma identification skills exceptional. Half of victims raised pets. Easy to track. Hairs everywhere. Know how much washing and cleaning of clothes required.

Male serial killer Anton evoked neat freak persona, almost

as if he vacuumed and steamed himself every single day, hour by hour, because trace evidence he knew to be his enemy and road to undoing. Voices, genderless, spoke to her.

"nature and stature evoked an easy prey appearance..."

"she walked as death trap garbage disposal..."

"sieve for scraps selection..."

"found no place to relax in her dark mind. Sought social interaction massage to mousy, emotive storm tiger..."

"her mind bounced along track, in train of steeled square wheels...all thoughts slowly grounded like coffee beans into ingredient for adrenaline..."

"yes...Saints inhabited Demon World, for what purpose uncertain; perhaps spy; perhaps observation; perhaps evil acts repented, to become burnt out of iniquity garbage pile; perhaps advisors to consult for insight into scurrilous phantasm of sentient mind or broken subconscious, pulling splinters from pocked skin, soul, being..."

"...limbo housed in-between spirits, window watchers, here for some time or just sprits dashed and dried and disappeared...to always love and care was still truncated time point in Demon World...; crash in, crash out..."

"Maybe killing binge required," she thought.

Thrash to death many on one dark morning, but some of

these punishments and revenges were too civil for evil. Some better concluded in existence of torture after thrashing when death acted only as victim relief. Humanoid perspective of truest pain resulted in healthy helping of eternal grief. She obliged such fears.

8

7

Hokum Smoke 'em Poke 'em

To become ruined by truth was difficult pill to swallow. Two female friends, friendly in more ways than one, sat at dark wooden table in speak-easy type restaurant. Ariadne wondered why she perceived much of this world like Old Earth domain. Perhaps it impressed her much. Soft music sounds dripped from fingertips of musician who tripped digits along guitar strings randomly yet in orderly manner.

She recognized each female from floral shop days ago few. Then, they could not keep bodies off each other when they came in, practically attached at respective hip bones. Handsy, each proceeded amidst one another, sliding, gliding, finger tipping, shoulder to hip dipping. Love dance in motion proceeded.

Ariadne laid trap. Side eye glances at blonde's face, lips, chin established invite. Blonde licked her lips while directly gazing into Ariadne's eyes. Shielded by front counter, emotive intensity struck Ariadne, level unexpected. Remained in control of brains, though.

Enjoyed feelings immensely. Brunette heat levels elevated

to point where she looked away to avoid revelation of her

disturbed mo. Two ticks later, blonde protruded long and hard her tongue towards Ariadne's eyes, in shadow of brunette's look away. Sneaky snuck in act, intentionally. Perhaps to spur emotions in brunette or avenge instance of previous betrayal or neglect. Blonde then waggled tongue tip; first slowly left; then slowly right; then skyward, slower; then downward towards heat of symbolic hellfire.

Large mirror on counter, strategically placed by Ariadne in design, to capture facial expressions and physical motions of customers for assessment of their intentions; confirmed brunette's abject displeasure. Brunette spied blithely every movement of blonde's tongue from beginning to end, in reflection reveal at rear windowed, floral arrangement display case. Nudge towards doom commenced. Job essentially finished. Ariadne's two randy customers managed remainder of scene as each perceived necessity to do so; in what manner, by what means. Only stage location needed for conclusion to performance.

"Going to Iron Bone tonight, we are," blurted brunette. Blonde retracted tongue extension before it completely lost silky saliva smoothness. Brunette attempted recovery of jealousy facial, but color crimson ruled in mirror reflection.

"Guaranteed fun," Ariadne said, masking tone of glee.

Later that evening, Ariadne waltzed into Iron Bone, captured glance from blonde. Ariadne picked up her takeout order, exited after elegantly placed hard glance at blonde. Brunette jealousy level aroused when blonde looked at Ariadne's rear end along route to front door. Jealousy at fever pitch mentally recorded by Ariadne.

Essentially, her work was done for these two.

They would start journey to their own respective ends. Knives out, from tabletop, rudely inserted into more voluptuous body portions of each; meaty thigh; elegant bicep; wiry stretched neck muscles. Butchery reigned in knife stroke virtuoso performance until each bloodied other into a final breath. No Gomwinds called. None needed. Each woman would serve as fresh meal for customers in attendance who gloriously witnessed spectacle of orchestrated blood drawing motions.

Ariadne rested against brick pocked exterior wall near front door. Slow turned and looked back, naturally, at interior dinner scene, through glistening evening moon colored window. Neon sign at top of window beamed "Iron Bone. Where customers choose menu." Soft music ambled together with patron light laughter sounds. To no one around, she pinched final nerve of moment, "So, what do you think? Is Paradise good place or bad place?" Ariadne thought about it, for bits of time. "I don't know. I just don't know." She tingled deep inside and didn't know why. Biological analysis of collected remains pended.

Upon return to flower shop, she rested, but not entirely.

Ariadne's time constraints became more pressing, upon her minds, as she schemed to complete each Mission Target goal. After Iron Bone affair, she took deep rest, almost cocooned, until all data she had absorbed during Training time began to coalesce into thoughts of more efficient plans. "Biological or chemical means of criminal Sentence completion for each Mission Target begged more efficient attention." Such thought poked at her psyche, hot and sharp and swift. Such anxiety moments helped her to focus, then discover, indirect physical efficiency quotient. Plant or implant death mechanism in or around each Target. Feasibility means depended on strengths and weaknesses of each.

Misty Memories, Wry Smiles Rye Dry

She tested her plan on Old man who unintentionally or accidentally murdered anyone who came to visit his house unannounced. Was he cursed? His house and yard and objects inside and out seemed to perpetuate killing events on purpose, based on Ariadne's case study data. Jealous house? Turned out one woman who generation ago died in house later returned as Spirit form. Ariadne developed connection between Him and Her: spouses of each, they were. Woman ghost spirit was very jealous of husband's perceived humanoid inter-actions.

He was still alive, old in age, and now resided in Nursing home. His spouse, Spirit Woman, killed anyone who visited house who she didn't know, since she imagined her male spouse engaged in affair with each, yet Old man spouse was clean as newly stripped bone. Ariadne located Old man spouse at Nursing home for terminally ill located in remote Prison town location. He had been convicted of all crimes and remained Button Hand Mission Target.

She Spoke with him about house machinations. Learned from Old man about his wife's killings, which he hid for years. Reason for his Prison world internment. He found victim bodies after wife intentionally led him to final resting places in house behind wall she obsessively performed drywall work upon; some buried under garden in back yard; others hidden in spare room unused in basement because her children moved out as she drove them away with her jealousy. Opportunity knocked at door. Ariadne answered it. Multiple Targets rumored to assemble.

She arranged meeting with local Gomwind Magistrate. Outside they ate, seated at round table, arm's length apart at local diner, in darkest part of city, just before midnight, when madness tones begged to commence orchestration. Conversation air quiet, as communication ensued telepathically, given their ethnic born abilities.

"Listen, little one," Gomwind Magistrate urged. Ariadne nodded respect. "I will keep watch over you, but alone, each of us must work. I am not allowed to further your Mission. Violates my oath."

"Understood."

Quiet became dotted in telepathic signal as city sounds, echoes of sounds, and bell tones of mischief rang.

"I have assured your safe entry. I will ensure your exit, in any form required." Nearby, commotion ensued. "I'm needed elsewhere," Gomwind Magistrate projected in thought to Ariadne. She understood since Mission picture began blaze into her head. "I will observe only," advised Gomwind Magistrate.

Misty Memories, Wry Smiles Rye Dry protocol popped into Ariadne's head. "That's one of my Missions."

Relevant Mission thoughts, targeted to this moment, collectively transferred amidst their consciences. At commotion scene she arrived.

"Cursed by mystery of longevity. Not too long ago to remember. Too long ago to forget." Memory Drop they each had captured. Their senses homed in onto relevant moments.

Nursing home Old man, recently escaped, approached by Younger man in shopping Mall who claimed to be Old man's son. Old man did not recognize him. Old man tried to get away, but then on-scene Gomwind Officer approached him and stated in robotic voice tones, "You have to go with this Younger man, he is trying to help you". Old man objected and became loudly verbal.

"I'll be right there," Ariadne tele-waved to Gomwind Officer. Officer didn't respond. Ariadne tried tele-wave again. No response. "Something not right," she surmised.

She swiftly entered Mall location, one block over from restaurant patio, worked undercover. Then, she received tele-wave message from Gomwind Magistrate.

"Mission Target Nursing Home Old man involved in altercation. Exercise caution." Ariadne responded, "Got it."

To detain Younger man, Ariadne entered picture, then calmed down Old man. Emotion slowly dripped from her pre-programmed psyche, in unprogrammed manner. Confused her, but she let it flow freely. She escorted away Old man to place of safety. She learned Old man was authorized Visitor, arrived to say goodbye to one of town's prisoners awaiting execution. But she wasn't convinced. She noticed apparition of woman hovering over scene. Her nuanced bio-detectors unable to identify apparition. She wondered if it was Old man's deceased spouse, creating more mischief even in her later stages of Spirit existence. Perhaps her purpose had become to string Old man along, like puppet, for her own amusement. Gomwind Magistrate tele-waved to Ariadne.

"Gomwind Officer fraud detected, in on

Younger man swindle, not real Gomwind Officer, changeling biology detected," her Gomwind Magistrate friend advised from his observation point. He further directed, "I will secure unauthorized Visitors per protocols."

"I see, and Younger man was scammer who had taken over Old man's financial accounts for profit," Ariadne added into thought recipe. Still, Old man, escorted back to Nursing Home, unable to escape his fate.

Dark Lady Shady

Touch. Touch important in humanoid and creature interactions. Helped develop communication amidst entities. Deception, also, touch became, when used for illicit purpose. Ariadne reviewed in her head Training Lesson data geared towards touch implications upon planning phase for next Mission. Doom hands and limbs loomed. Soft fury of deception fur tingled upon her psyche.

Dark Lady cheated regularly on her current spouse. She had murdered some prior spouses along her cruel machination path. Her end time had arrived per Target list.

So, Ariadne took place of intended victim

current spouse, in standard humanoid Changeling mode of two upper limbs and two lower limbs, and one penis composed of urethra traversed by corpus spongiosum tipped by meatus. Prior to spouse moment of conjugal visit, Gomwind Magistrate had carted him away to assure wronged spouse's safety. Ariadne allowed herself to become imprisoned in Dark Lady basement, chained at wrist and ankles. Once Dark Lady convinced bindings secure, and after she had ascended stairs to upper floor to further prepare for death moments, Ariadne prepared for vile ending of Dark Lady life story.

Ariadne coaxed Dark Lady back into basement bowels, feigned agony and fear and pain sounds loudly. Slid and twisted, she did, her limbs from chains, and waited for Dark Lady to descend wooden-hard, dank steps into basement bowels, amidst black and chunky bugs of many antenna which clung to rock walls. Ariadne resisted sucking in some of bugs. Would break her humanoid assumed cover. Thoughts of such snacks stimulated her.

Ariadne wasn't terribly certain what type anatomy she had invaded during Changeling mode. Penis tool seemed too long, thickish; banged into her thighs like bell chimes. Pit pat. Pit pat. She blended into shade of wall darkness as Dark Lady touched foot pads to cement floor.

Dark Lady looked around, surprised at scene she surmised as spouse sexual game. "Oh! You naughty!" Her voice screeched, scratched stone walls. Then, in lower provocative tone, "Figured out how to escape, I see." Ariadne remained silent, so long, she noticed silence stabbed at Dark Lady mind.

Slow and stealth maneuvers Dark Lady commenced against darkness whole. Chill in dank air caused her exposed plump parts to jiggle, uncontrollably. Forwards, sideways, backwards she moved her frame, one unsteady leg at each movement, foot searching for stable position against sudden strike upon her anatomy. She seemed to exhibit some kind of radar function but wave lengths not audible.

At varied moments, Ariadne extended her hands from darkness shroud in which she hid, and transformed them into thick, sharp tentacles, readied to stab, stake, or impale as appropriate against Dark Lady's body angle.

Dark Lady assumed position directly in front of Ariadne form, turned around to expose her back, round buttocks, and hard thick legs, adorned in mesh red stockings, upper body in lacey dangling's dark, still blind to her ultimate demise moment. Ariadne thrusted forward spear sharp tentacles, one puncture at each thrust, into anatomical portions of Dark Lady body. Last few pokes and thrusts could bring any number of results. Then, one movement elicited moan, then groan, then silence. Heaving sounds evolved from silence, then Dark Lady body spasms, as if stimulated by pain.

"My goodness your skills have advanced. So, I must ask, who or what are you?" Ariadne remained, inside insolent darkness silence. She felt tightness and tension increase around tentacles she had invaded into Dark Lady body. Ariadne's stabs had missed their appropriate death inducing marks. Dark Lady not injured, merely sensually stimulated. Ariadne then unleashed all of her tentacles in frantic mash against Dark Lady anatomy.

Each strike seemed to sensually stimulate Dark Lady further and frustrate Ariadne further. Game was on now.

"Run out clock," Ariadne thought. Extended unleashed tentacles and used them to block all anatomy holes from top to bottom by insertion thereto. Shook, she did, Dark Lady more and more and more. Shudders gradually receded from Dark Lady's body, until rest beckoned, either rest of breath or life's death, Ariadne remained unsure. She didn't want to make huge mess; still needed biological samples for analysis Mission phase. She began absorption of bio and chem Dark Lady elements through tentacles bores and invasive spore injections. Suction phase started. Dark Lady remained limp, now as anatomical deflation into more stable material form.

After extinguishment of Dark Lady, who exuded sexual identity unknown, Ariadne receded from Changeling form and completed collection of relevant biologic materials for proof of kill and future analysis, then snooped around on above floor room areas. She found small, lightweight, and curious mechanical device. Difficult to hold, it was. Clicked largest button. Wall screen transformed into visual and audible light projections. Viewed and listened.

Her Mission Target was apparently rather anal about her electronic system. Kept detailed history of acquaintances, including photographs, voice to voice contacts, physical interactions. Ariadne's body tingled inside and out at enticement of knowledge nuggets. Data treasure trove to explore and catalogue into next Assignments. Found veritable outlines of Dark Lady encountered character portraits.

Ariadne recorded data in her appropriate brain boxes. Were these data treasures friends or future victims of Miss Dark Lady Shady? She plugged into her brain box info for any matches. Bingo. She didn't need all these hits. Saved info for future Assignments, but some results matched her specific Assignment Marks.

She conversed between brains. "Tell me what is there. Why do I need such data? When? Let me catch needed or greeted greed so long as deed deceived desperately done."

Odd prayer, she thought, but not to argue with brains, she learned. Discretionary tools already baked into data pudding. Eat it. Excrete it, as relevant and necessary. Or die.

Beauty she found in some Marks, of varied degrees; in appearance, demeanor, mannerisms, intonations of speech; and especially in aroma. Smell. Sweet temptation. In some instances, gripped her soul like long-nailed, ripping claw. Data boxes in this world provided much aroma samples. She sniffed each into her anatomy and biology and chemistry for later reference.

Again, smell primarily stung; swung terrible nasal tune. Voice inflection and tone could master same trick. All moments alike jabbed hard into her guttural area. Her inexperience allowed no Instructional help. Some waters must become charted blind in order to navigate path. Reprogram. Advance.

Danger dripped from such moments. Mental energy used

during learning process truncated perspective view until new trenchant revelation firmly formed.

She consoled herself in reward factor. Any spare blood, bone, sinew or flesh, post Assignment completion, reverted to her for consumption, as prize.

There were days when everyone and everything looked like edible delights. Ave Maria already. She liked that thought. Came across it in Old Earth humanoid history Training. An old history of archaic knowledge and extinct Beings, yet to latch onto it by song sounds struck chords in her soul of memorable merit. Sounds of Dead calls. Musky aroma of loneliness tomes.

Strange Magic, Range Tragic

"Sometimes you must punch Death's face and watch it bleed," she surmised. Her offer to babysit for adult male floral shop customer, personage mysterious yet tugged towards her psyche, was accepted. Upon arrival at designated destination, she found open door to tiny house. After looking around outside, sniffing varied wind current aromas nearby, she ventured inside. Tiny house merely represented entry to larger, deeper abode below ground. Below ground, through a long corridor, she found two children.

Words unspoken, they walked together along

passage which opened into dark commercial Mall. Followed children who stopped intermittently to rest amid shadows, then continued further along and purchased tickets to Movie, entered theatre amidst many beings, some calm, most unquiet verbally. Two humanoids, men she determined based on aroma and demeanor, who seemed to search for seats, perhaps in ruse fashion as something else on their minds appeared apparent.

Ariadne slowed her mind to scan their faces and recognized one as designated Mission Target. He argued with table of patrons until one stood and walked away. Mission Target seated himself. His right-hand squirmed in pants pocket.

Long-legged brown spider type creature, size of dinner plate, dropped out of ceiling darkness propelled from web strand which glistened thick amidst movie screen light reflection. Ariadne twitched and swished spider creature away unsuccessfully as it collected upon her arm web-like.

Creature struck her left hand on top portion which caused it to morph into her natural tentacle tip state, out of nervous involuntary reaction. She pulled her tentacle away from spider attack prongs, but its legs hardened and swelled in thickness, turned green like asparagus shoots, especially at point of attack.

More and more she pulled against spider's leg grips as they hardened and extended pins from legs. Top half of Ariadne's tentacle started transforming into clear and luminescent jelly-like substance. Eventually, female Usher rushed over and told Ariadne to relax, then Usher extended her own fingers, like boney spine tips mounted to a brush handle, and massaged hardened spider legs. Spider's legs began to soften. Spider head, now hard as rock, receded from deadly tentacle nip and looked up at Usher.

Ariadne sensed intense feelings upon her back. She turned and to her left noticed man who visited her floral shop earlier. Perhaps he used these children as props to lure his potential victims. She wondered if he had been following her movements in neighborhood, and if so, for how long.

Brickhouse Bastard, Gym Dandy Rescue

Her Mall movie theatre encounter continued in presence of suspicious man Mission Target she scoped there. Humanoid man beast, he was, suffered anger problems. Gradually, his temperament of anger increased, until he achieved an ever-angry status. He must learn to control it or lose all humanity and morality in himself. He failed.

Each degree of anger impulse created thickened skin, hardened heart, where morality problems enhanced. His gradual inability to feel, mentally and physically, doomed him to strict punishments for indiscretions violent perpetrated upon those who he encountered. Banished to prison world of Ariadne's Mission Assignment location.

Mentally, he had descended into levels of hell reserved only for personalities like himself. Such ailment, control of self, cursed many demons. Blight upon culture. Struggled for self-control. Anger blunted strength. Allowed it to spread weak thin, in shards, instead of in streams directed fine.

In such Hell reserved only for himself, forced he was to watch movies of his own memories, installed by micro-chip through sensory nodes of his unique anatomy. Essentially, doctors determined such scheme as means to reprogram his thoughts.

First good thoughts when he helped others to straighten their own paths, then mistakes self-perpetrated as caution markers.

Slowly, his observations of others' mistakes latched onto his mind more firmly and sabotaged psychological cure efforts. His subconscious rejected such curative efforts and fired them back into his conscious mind.

There he stood, tall and high, rock hard, unable to move, yet alive as ever, to suffer aches and pains of no movement, until his sentence completion date, many years into future. Eyes of all creatures and beings sentenced to this Prison world countenanced his anatomy statuesque, unmovable, inescapable, in village square walks, located not terribly far from Ariadne's floral shop.

She too passed by on evening walks, forced to ponder his predicament, as all others of this world encountered same stone statue of self-imposed, interminable incarceration. His enslavement to stone essence, immovable, yet exposed in all of his demon glory, served, whether he appreciated it or not, as reminder of who not to emulate. He was fed regularly, barely, by Prison workers.

Ariadne checked list of Inmates coded into her Mission Task register. Loaded data and reviewed it. This inmate had always wanted to look bigger. His head was oversized in relation to his body. Lifted weights but still didn't get much more muscle size. Refused use of drugs or steroids.

In early adulthood, plagued by severe migraines. Taken to hospital for tests. Learned he had registered overly high testosterone levels, and multiple old broken and healed bones were discovered. Suffered injuries, he had, but never sought treatment or hospitalized as such injuries he considered nuisance pains. Significant shots of adrenaline plagued him almost daily, almost super humanoid in nature when subjected to extended times of stress.

Unable to rescue himself, he remained on display, only in visage, unnamed, unspoken, not even breaths of his own lungs audible to passersby, as reminder for others to rescue themselves, before too late date arrived. Functional obsolescence punishment had replaced his curse of eternal anger. Perhaps Target she spotted in theatre was Changeling. If so, why did it emulate statue figure? Puzzlement time she had no use for. Onward.

Dumpster Dive Hive

Walking on street one night, she came across creature sitting on sidewalk edge, near alley waste bins, not far from her closed floral shop. It did not move upon her closeness arrival. Male or female or bionomic creature traits she could not surmise, but troubled it seemed, shaking erratically, balled up as if in a snail shell. She pestered sound towards it. Movement stopped. Face of creature now visible. Horrid appearance. Difficult to discern face features. Sometimes multiple eyeballs popped forward from skin surface. Clothing style pedestrian, dark, somewhat shredded as if overused.

She noticed this creature previously. Specific anatomical traits indecipherable. Perhaps darkness provided energy to it.

No words involved in their common space exchange, but her mind jiggled somewhat as if creature tried communication through wavelengths. She tried to tap into those waves until signal refined to her hearing.

"Hello. Do not belong here. My world, all I have known, darkness. Light hurts me. Not sure why here."

Ariadne wondered how she could help creature. Her effort to identify method plan not successful. Perhaps creature was merely lost, and she could help it along to proper path.

"No," creature responded telekinetically. Comforted, she became since creature telekinetic response indicated communication possible. She wondered what service she could possibly provide. It spoke to her again, in tone somewhat pleading.

"Help me find way back to eternal darkness of my home."

Ariadne responded in same demoniac manner. No lip movement required. No eye movement needed. No body emulation warranted.

"Perhaps if I knew your origin, where you came from, or how you came to arrive here. I could help."

"I don't know," creature thought-waved back to her.

"May I tap your mind thoughts?"

Creature lowered head. Transparent outer layer of skin peeled backwards slowly, gradually, like onion skin, until hollow space remained. Ariadne tilted her head to one side, confused, then realized nudges to her brains began jiggle movement. Such electric emanations, unfamiliar to her, worked some magic into her mind; massaged it; penetrated pudding of it. Hollow space was alive, invisible to her naked vision, yet quite active in biologic activity on microscopic level.

She traveled mentally along same wavelength path as creature, yet she sensed other wavelength movements along it she could not identify. Translation of audible signals in wavelengths proved difficult.

Developed name, place, method of restoration, impossible to detect, as if creature's mind had been selectively wiped. Still, she discerned resurrection as only method of proper restoration acceptable in creature's home culture. Creature agreed he must become extinguished to achieve an aspect of origin return; find path through absolute nothingness to find proper darkness origin realm.

"I recall dreadful things. Things done by me in darkness. Required to search for my soul in my mind, amid thoughts. Believe I fell off right tracks."

She became confused about right tracks. Never

had she learned of such Being existence parameters as creature's mind emitters displayed, during her Training sessions. She sensed no danger to herself, but in Training she recalled when she was most calm and collected in situational Mission Path testing, even slight variations in her perception model of task calculations stimulated caution nodes to activate throughout her body. She began to understand and identify this moment with creature as such an example, but to avoid activation of creature's flight fear, she used her right brain to inject calming serum into her left brain, in hope it would allay creature's suspicions.

Her stratagem worked to some degree. Creature's muted

wavelengths were activated by cause of inability to further probe Ariadne's brain cavities. She discovered hives of wavelengths in creatures thoughts, segregated into varied action paths.

Suddenly, an appendage of creature reached out towards her, from underneath ragged cloth of body covering. She almost did not notice, but still noticed too late. Appendage of creature touched her lower body clothing and would not let go.

It tried to scratch through her clothing and gain access to

her skin covering. She felt tingles in her lower extremities. She then became rigid for moments, unexpectedly, which created recoiling of creature's appendage tip.

"What are you doing?" She transmitted. No response in creature's wavelengths detected by her.

Deflation commenced in creature's form, until all that remained was wrinkled, pasty goo. She guessed it had resurrected into a different existence plane. Origin plane unidentified in her Mission Training catalogue.

Imagination Cake

Fascination B & D Club, in name evoked emotive stimulus. Each sentient organism, of varied sizes and shapes and marks sore, bore facial masks, adorned by savage senses of deceptions past, cosmetically implanted, pasted onto facade of frantic and anxious remembering's past. Anticipation stimulants sounded from Trope John Jung, musician from whom hope's horn sprung, emitted sensuous impressions.

Ariadne's feet touched ground as felled rose

petals soft while sidewalk poet over invisible speakers strummed song verbal "do not be angry, do not be mean, let 'em live, and laugh, and learn, and scream." Last words always count.

She allowed herself to become captured in rhythms. Dangerous course ensued. All entities sought control, over self, condition, outer forces. Spider snake trappings hung everywhere. Their web strands glistened amidst interior glow of grotesquely shaped light ornaments mounted from ceiling and along walls. Intricate beauty nets they sewed, then descended from onto many scantily cladded humanoid and other creatures floor revelers in spun strands. Descended, they did, to capture all, as victims, less one. Ariadne. Her body scent she had adjusted to evoke aroma of spider snakes as defense against tug of elegant attack ballet. She waved tentacles at spider snakes, in appreciation, on her way out.

Reign Pain

She didn't know what would happen, but it would happen, nonetheless. Short in stature male, he was, who entered Ariadne's floral shop. His stated purpose, in banal tone, to look for birthday gift, at least, that's how he audibly broke ice to open encounter door. No further words needed to express delineation of his needs.

Aroma and physical actions provided all communication

methods needed from this point forward. She identified him by smell, and physical size, as Mission Target epitomized by acts of forcible, physical subjugation.

His aroma did not strike her as enticing, due to species differences, yet she masked such reticence She reached one tentacle downward under service countertop and pushed lever to auto lock shop front door, then signaled to him from her nasal twitches an interest languished deep within her. Such action by her visibly stimulated his nasal passages to respond in kind. He knew females of his species would recognize his needs and purpose, so he seemed convinced, at least enticed. She realized he needed resistance from her in order to assume proper stimulation level. She began meek, victim appearance. "I understand," she voiced lowly as she facially emulated resignation. "Do as I say, changeling." She bowed her head; wondered how he came to think of her as changeling.

Each of them moved softly, calmly into alley just outside rear shop entrance. Cool breeze tunneled alley path. She could feel wind vibrations rolling along alley borders of stone walls on either side, each stone wall abutted by flora and fauna of sweet fragrance tinged by dank ground surface odor.

Slowly they transformed, two-legged humanoid male into four-legged canine appearance, and she eight-legged creature into four-legged figure of plump and sumptuous bounty. Each body part of transformation either loosened or tightened strands of clothing, but not to point of ripping or tearing. His jaws became drool-dripping jowls. His fingertips distended grotesquely; reflected simplest and dimmest of light fragments.

Ariadne's transformation allowed for her to slide from her clothing constraints, but his changes created constraints, yet his clothing design allowed for supple metamorphosis.

Bestial ballet commenced. Each sniffed other, nose to hindquarters, in confirmation of orgasmic meal about to become served. Alley behind flower shop served as quaint encounter plate amid hardened gardens.

Her back hunched as he pushed his prickly loin horn into her moist hindquarters. His search angle commenced in earnest as means to coax pleasure elixir into her warm, soft innards. His persistent forward push startled her to extent of trauma. She dug her claws into alley ground surface in order to remain rigid, but his thrusts pushed her head into bushes, then up against stone wall. Her paws strained to grip ground. Her head ached from wall bumps. Unable to sustain canine creature form, she began to transfer back into her natural physical form.

He became irritated and frustrated and thrusted forth harder and faster. If she let him continue, he would eventually lose enough energy enough for her to whirl around and pounce upon him to finish Mission Target assignment. Eventually her pain receptors subsided, numbed through gross amounts of his repetitive thrusts.

His ejaculation thrusts commenced. Training Manual indicated Target victim in such status would lose hold of visual acuity. She allowed transformation to her natural form and whirled around while he remained plugged into her octopussoir. In struggle, they twisted and turned, until she commanded superior position. Upon his face she pressed her loins while his jism rocketed into far wall. As it streamed downward, she suffocated him. His foreclaws scratched her back severe and deep. She winced while her biological defense mechanisms dulled pain darts. Victim's prying, prayed forth and long nails spewed blood, tissue and skin like raindrops as they splashed into alley puddles.

His last throes of life receded. Her biological elements collection commenced.

Crock Lawyer

Legal Prosecutor Target Mark, no name provided in profile details, but his biology collection helped her home in on his daily machinations, took payoffs to let violent criminals escape prosecution. Ariadne investigated and learned of whole group of prosecutors, defense lawyers and Judges involved in monetary kick-back schemes. Pay to play or rot away.

One evening when group hosted alleged Charity

Ball, Ariadne invited herself, spread her hypnotic elixir, then coaxed elixated lawyers to accidentally set Hall on fire from cigars, cigarettes, and lighters thereof. All of those in Hall attendance had previously engaged in illegal depravity. Wait staff and other workers were excepted as she allowed for their quick escape.

Judges, lawyers burned alive, feeling flames flickers, but physically entranced, moved around like zombies in and amid arrow tip sharpened heat. Their cocksure mannerisms dropped like ashen flies. Sprinklers turned on but their metal pinwheels spun of old age and pipes corroded pressure lacked sustainable projection, so water sprinkled out slowly, not enough to douse ultimate and complete conflagration.

"Goodbye", she whispered. Wondered whether she would ever happen to see them again, and she was not quite sure why such thought possessed her in this moment.

An unknown male demon voice spoke to her. She recognized voice tonality but could not recall time or place or such experience moment in either brain.

"I'll let you in on little secret. All-Seeing All-Knowing God, it is no different than those created by Omniscience. Groups and Clans created and encouraged to thrive, to ward off against each other, declare victory or suffer defeat, all for amusement of Omniscient One as simply amusement matters. Sadly, enough time in humanoid years hasn't been granted for these competing groups to figure out such schematic skullduggery."

She imagined her Controller's report summary for Mission Task work, except voice spoke to her in male demon tone.

She wondered to where was her mind traveling.

"As her Controller, I write these words. Unfortunately, I begin to realize Ariadne has become tired of Training Tasks, Mission worn even before her first assignment. Seems our Peripheral made mistake, despite Bio-Related mechanism principle. Each regeneration of her spirit creates concern for me. A faulty spirit was primary death of organism generated. Perhaps she isn't one to continue this path. She hasn't learned to control her mind. It rips too easily, frequently, shredded flag blowing."

Most Buttons failed on their first mission,

unable to complete all mark extinguishments and then, if they survived, Controller relegated them to lower echelon of dimensional activity, never again allowed rise to next competence Level regardless of competence skills developed. Humiliation punishment. Incentive for successful completion methodology. Failure punished. Exceptions minimal. Some were extinguished in process through error or bad intelligence provided from start. Planned obsolescence. First mission always most dangerous. Preternatural flaw in temperament, a caused hesitation, could lead to self-extinguishment as type of regret suicide.

Science and religion of this environment were not unlike many sentient worlds. Each gradually developed through observation and rumination. Blanks of thought and experience became filled in by reason available at evolutionary stages of development; later revised sometimes in bloody coups; stamped upon culture; further analyzed or modified depending on social rights permitted publicly; yet, always an underbelly of contrary thoughts persisted like rocks buried at bottom of slow moved stream waters. Error in collective consciousness created periods of darkness and extinction of minds, bodies, souls.

No matter. Rewrites ruled days. Yet, rewrites and revisions devoid of complete information and data resulted in continuous false conclusions. Such conclusions masked Missions and works of Button Hands and their Controllers. Convenient deceit curtains and crafty veils of false flags walled off ultimate discovery of Ariadne's home world. Spies and lies and devils' eyes, they were, cloaked in undiscoverable mystery solutions, then sewn into thoughts as deserved victim lures.

Maturity migration generally tied to age progression, but many humanoids and otherwise never attained such level of sentient consumption existence tactics. Pity. Peace reigns in mind at such Level. Darkness shades down pulled, otherwise. No pill, or drug or drink or food for maturity attainment. Passed time and growth intention, mentally and spiritually combined in necessary required measures must be mastered. To catch an empty air easier in task. Thoughts fired at her projectile-like. Ouch. Failed meaning captures became boring, humdrum, faded. Immune to it she became.

Tattered threads of try flayed about her psyche, only calmed by windless seizes of stop. Stop hurt. Mind blank cope even hurt as blind blur.

To not know was worse than to not wonder. Wonder was drug she looked for. Her Training search forged frustrations large especially when blank spaces along path. Obliterate blanks or become swallowed in them. Useless endeavor as each knowledge moment acquired, many more questions born. Less sentient creature existed much easier. How, what, when, where, why, not an issue for insentient.

She wondered if she was not able to kill anymore once she believed love possibility existed towards another living creature. Falling in love with serial killer man, or demon. She was not quite sure about his origin story just yet. Was he humanoid man or another demon from rival clan? Perhaps his aroma, science enhanced, he used as lure.

After each kill failure of her Mission, she later learned of, by means of electronic or paper media or sidewalk whispers in town, someone or something had beaten her to punch and had offed some of her botched Marks. Botched in sense Marks were killed before she could even conduct her Mission Task on them. Local news media sources characterized these murders as accidents. Means of death reported but her senses laid unsure.

Apparently, loneliness evolved as subset of some general emotions she chose for Assignment mold. Love confused her. Purpose she could not find for it. Floating clouds and mists, it was. Puffy. Plump. Spread thin. Painted as haberdashery in sky.

Temptations. Male subject's smell, eyes, hair movement in wind, clothes of dress, muscles long and lean, tall stature, magical hands, no marks on his skin, not much body hair.

Ariadne knows there are always Watchers, some-where, sent by Demon clan leaders to verify Mission Mark Task completed. Her brains counseled, "Tyrant in our midst."

End Protocol

Festered dread infected her psyche. Time ran short, laps to go. Masquerade Ball drained her of too much energy. At second floor bedroom in floral shop, she reviewed Target Mark Hit List. Scheme to encounter remaining Targets may work some time saver magic. Plotted, she did, to bring them together, except for big fish Anton, as means to trigger Mission end.

Hunger plagued her. As youngling, food hunger prevailed. Basic need of all kind. As food became more available, some wants befell her as temptation curse. But hunger demanded many moments. To not feed meant to suffer many, many moments.

As food for her needs increased in frequency so too tug of wants grew. Times of satiated appetite allowed for cogitation mysterious as soul and mind competed for attention as next hunger plague; hunger for knowledge and understanding. Her education, from beginning of such routine, tickled in her much thought and steady rumination of question and answer. More questions than answers resulted.

Once she arrived at age when food hunger had become

afterthought stimulated by overabundance, plague of wants horribly asserted dominance in her mind; agitated her soul; distracted vengeance feelings to front of her meditations. Wanting needy reigns. Needing necessary drains.

As for love, not an issue. Never concerned about

it. Not relevant to her reason for existence. Stories of no good worth end, she learned in her Training. Her Demon clan was not conceived in love, from love, by love, except to manipulate Targets. Her training provided no sources for love concepts in her language. She searched other languages, but no findings. She heard stories of love, verbally shared, as in rhymes or jokes, but nothing put to writings or drawings or art. If such concept of mutual feelings between two or more sentient entities existed, evidence of such was not preserved in her Clan.

She wondered if her Mission Task destination could provide enlightenment. Eventually, she searched "Tools", and found love identified as such, but peculiar tool it was, and apparently not considered useful or necessary in many species of humanoids or lesser sentient life forms.

Needy, greedy, seedy, weedy growth among all humanoid populations and cultures entwined together. Sellers, buyers, hucksters, liars among subsets thereof flourished. Scoundrels, mongrels, wranglers, pustules poisoned and nourished existence parameters. Light of day exposed, revealed such humanoid machinations. Dark of night reposed, yet even stronger clutched control and monstrously overcame day's light. Solace existed exactly nowhere, anywhere; had become forged and cooked, and once cooled, sat deceivingly humble amidst merchandised wares. Old Earth author's Poe or Lovecraft or King could not have devised ever crueler or soulless beasts.

For every rose, there hid amongst ground soil, poison sumac. She decided she had beaten hell out of such thoughts. Tired her mind out. Wrenched it of sentient tonality. Humans moved slower than dogs, in body, if not mind. Stopped in her tracks like fashioned faux pas. Pains of body posed to her less concern than pains of mind.

Are some of the murders result of plant life? Large Venus fly trap types? Can Ariadne imitate a plant that can catch, capture, consume a victim? Similarly, can she emulate an animal or bird for same purpose? To lure prey, then capture, then consume? Purpose of her job at flower shop? She created flower shop in vacant store front. Or perhaps she took over after killing owner and impersonated owner as Button Hand Mark task, or lied about taking over for owner while owner out of town? She began to wonder if these Tasks drove her mad. Perhaps each kill released victim's defense mechanism intended to infect her biology.

"Am I experimental kill machine?" Time to sleep.

9

8

Anton Moves In, Two Brains Too Many

Anton stalked her. Wind he felt blow from one avenue,

but flowers outside floral shop, on display for customers, blew in opposite direction. He sensed something wrong because he had been stalking Ariadne, Marked her as his victim, even while killing others. Then when he believed he had figured out her patterns and actions, he moved in for kill.

He telepathically tapped into Ariadne's wavelength, but it was too late. She used her spiritual force to reverse all of his actions. And now he knew. Steamed, he became, as realization arose that she had bested him during stalk maneuvers.

She knew he was serial killer, just another

demon sent by rival demon Clan to sabotage, steal Ariadne's Marks for themselves. One look at his true essence could kill. Resurrection not capable as inner core of soul is turned to ashes. Ariadne possessed same power. Which would survive unveiling?

"I know what you are?"

"Really."

"I've seen you kill."

"So, you know."

He stared at her, into her eyes bored deeply his vision.

She responded. "Do you like what can be seen?"

Respond, he did not. Silence took hold in air. Silence before death, she recognized. Hollow. Portended echoes of calamity and extermination.

"I know your history, genealogy, essence formicatory scheme." He glared.

"I know some nothing of you." She smiled.

Enhanced glare betrayed rhythm of his stare. He serenaded her, caustically.

"Whatcha' gonna do? Whatcha' Gonna do? Whatcha' Gonna Dooooo......?"

Boymore

No hulks, no bulks in this dimension. Concentrated energy ruled and reigned. Sucking pipe dreams kept hope alive, as dead as dead could be. Death evolved from life. seeds remained. Even in death, life force remained. sterilized hope remained hope. Past moments dead. New moments beckoned, stripped of imagination. Still, imagination remained juice of life mix. Jet streams were evidence of life blasts past.

She had designated him "Boymore" in her analytical brain

side, as further classification stealthily eluded her. Not sure whether Training gaps or intended elusion tracks, Management induced, broke her understanding trail path. Hardly, she thought, had she discovered new species on her first Mission. Yes.

She knew Management had their favorites and schemed against each other to sabotage efforts. They knew she knew. So be it. Her life at stake determined course choices. Every path led to terminal failure.

She watched him, Boymore, run and play. Death plants unable to do such activity, yet somehow, he learned in this creature environment. Adaptable, he was. Had learned to shape his lower stalk roots into pads, like feet.

"Look, Ariadne, look!."

She looked.

"I learned it! I learned it!"

Amazed, she was. Didn't think he could do it at all, much less this soon. Amusement it was, learning journey, yet somehow, he turned it into skill test, and passed.

Burst sound she heard. Boymore was gone. "What happened?" She wondered. She got up, walked toward sound, no visible cause found. Walked more, to locate evidence of sound. Then, in flash point, heard she frequencies. Honed into them she tried, more than ever.

Her senses homed in on clues, yet resistance blocks smashed into her. Frustrated she became. Mysteries didn't elude her, couldn't elude her. Allow it, she would not. It had taken her while to find these thought seeds in her head, and now someone, something, some creature was trying to take it away from her.

Ripped from her physical touch; torn from her psyche analysis. An ally future, Boymore could become. Flash point extinguished. Understanding escaped her to point she needed emotional brain lasso, flung it outward, then pulled it back into her mind essence, but capture remained elusive, and penning up such thoughts, temporary.

Boymore, rare specimen, not encountered in her Mission

Training. Could not have been Target for her; perhaps for another Button Hand. At least such thoughts badly escaped from her attitude grasp. First time ever she needed something, someone, in such desperate yet meaningless manner. Realized, did she, meaningless could not become conclusion, regardless of Training. Emotion tug too great for controlled resistance walls.

Love had become born in her, for Boymore. Filial, or parental in nature, analytical brain identified, but source still eluded further analysis. Yet, far away in her brains, analysis had ensued, continued, and eventually led to one, only one conclusion. Boymore had not inadvertently or biologically or necessarily extinguished itself. Exterior, outer influence mechanism was cause.

Find cause, she must. Such thoughts blinded her

analysis path now. Realize she didn't, her physical path remained on course towards origin point of Boymore disappearance event. Strange breathing, she experienced, in company of increased intensity. Brain analysis ensued. Musical tones interrupted, then words formed into emotional brain. Her favored song sounds released, eased softly.

"friendship lost. loneliness found. cause elusive. turn thoughts around. away from chaos. misery fly. sounds muffled. visions spied. haze. blaze. numb. gums dry. emotions fly."

Her limbs flailed outward, downward, upward.

"drown, gag. torn, hag. mist, bag. drain, drag. gravity lost. depravity found. turn, turn. turn around."

Long and lean shadow escaped in her lateral vision corner.

Another had been present when boymore extinguishment

event happened. Suspect. Suspect analysis commenced, automatically, drastically, hastily, fantastically amidst each brain, until conclusion connections became forged. Shredded nonsense emotions permitted see, think clearer.

Crushed, she did, biological and sound wave distractions. Air around her became powdery in destruction detritus. Leeched into her thoughts came sounds preternatural. Birth sounds. Death moans. Sense certain eluded her mind. Wondered, she did, whether her brains had been invaded by exterior life force to push her off cliff of analysis certainty.

Meditation required, as mental connections for conclusion certainty evaded her grasp. She continued to collect into analytical brain, allowing some evidence to collate and merge into emotional brain as needed, to keep analytical brain clear. she would re-analyze later, in safe haven environment, but now concerns regarding shadow figure interruption became primary. At least, survival extinct kicked her hard towards such path. stealth mode encapsulated she. Enhanced body armor activated instinctively.

Always, there twisted, thread found available to be further

flayed in search of sensible sentience. When she finished identifying most viable and sentient life form drift, she followed it.

Big Fish

"Welcome back."

She nodded towards Anton's attention sound.

"Odd, is it not, you were assigned to this planet-oid, in this Dimension?"

She feigned confusion.

"I am not Class One Entity," he bragged.

"No, you are not," she acknowledged through brain wave communication. He shook like waves in pond spattered by leaf detritus fallen from above.

"You will not survive this Mission." His tone sounded certain.

"No, I will not." Her agreement pleased him.

"No worries?" He grinned wide. Ugly wide.

"You will not, also," she intoned, in soft silence of knife turned dagger penetration.

"Oh. Ooh, such succulent temptation. Yes, I can taste it."

"Enjoy," her feigned boredom tone rang.

"Sabotage or camouflage," he brain-waved back to her.

"The weakness of your civilization is evident."

"Enlighten me, if you will." She sent back such

thought in mist cloud, so he would need to search for each syllable.

Brain drains in process.

"Gender has been biologically engineered out of your humanoid gene pool."

"Sexual proclivities have been mixed together in order to

weed out biological bias." She surmised he would know such. Confused look towards his visage, she glanced, pushing his sentience to oblivious edge.

"I am from same gene pool as you. I escaped such madness, over time."

"And now, you take pride in mocking such cultures."

"With great joy."

Sedentary silence spread cloak-like upon moment's atmosphere.

"You have needed Training in how to act like male, or female, or neither."

"All beings need such Training," she noted.

"Not in sub-worlds. Biological, physiological, serological, and chemical cauldrons of life evolve naturally."

"Not necessarily rationally. Energy, power acquisition, dominance, determine such worlds."

He was not amused.

"Precisely." He intoned, emotionless in manner. Her next intellect offering response irritated him further.

"Evolution is process of time. We have added to mix, sentient, not accidental, evolution. Speeds process."

"Yes, it does. Yet, all weakness not eliminated. Bias of creator can never be weeded from process."

"And so now, we have you."

"Choice still rules, all."

"Yes. Yes, it does."

"Even those not instructed in choice management make choices."

"For better or worse?"

"There is no better or worse in evolution. There is only evolution. Process is purpose."

Cauldron of thoughts among them began to stir in each mind and coalesce into their collective consciousness. Evolution in process. Ariadne's analytical brain concluded such interaction results uncertain. She realized no error permitted. Either traceable mess or complete biological cleanup needed.

Her calm seemed to irritate. Waves of it she poured upon his presence. He betrayed his fear to her. Their eyes, of uncommon anatomy, did not normally blink, yet he blinked. It was then she knew the depth of his fear. Dread poured from his essence as thick syrup. Their mutual mind waves scattered, traced, escaped, regrouped until each became entrapped, entwined. Each realized common ethnic bonds between them of mixed level proportions and ratios: Gomwind, Oni.

"I know everything of your Mission," their flowed brain thoughts mutually waved, then ricocheted. His wave choked her. And his immediate physical presence arrived.

He pounced upon her unsuspecting body; laid upon her like Old Earth humanoid cowboys wrestled castrated bulls. His knees pressed against her upper body sides. His butt bounced upon her lower rib cage, pushing air out of her mouth. Her pain sensors gradually suppressed feeling to remain conscious, but her initial panic became titillation in her loins. What followed next teased her mind. Such feelings were foreign to her being. She allowed them to migrate throughout her anatomy.

His dual brains shouted wavelengths, to no one in particular, it seemed, "There is no destiny, for anyone. Fool's game, it is, to search such paths. Foul dream streams flow to nowhere." Such thoughts she had never considered. Irrelevant to her purpose, she surmised.

"Purpose! Purpose! You have no purpose." His thought words water-felled into a serene liquid pool. Rumination did not seem his best skill, from her ears to her mind. Possessed, he seemed, through his faults or another's, she was not sure. Did it really matter?

She withdrew tentacles from her humanoid encased arms. Her tormentor began to hammer his fists down upon her limbs. Shattered pieces of arms splintered into air. He did not seem to notice, clouded by his own dank fury. She made herself smaller, retracting in the tiny void of human doll masque. Then she struck, after his energy had waned, at source most vulnerable within her range, and plunged one tentacle which she rapidly expanded as it entered his lowest vulnerable extremity.

His body began to shake as moans of singular grief penetrated pain threshold. No creature or other being emitted such sound in Training Manual sessions. Unable to analyze properly, at this moment, understandable identification origins, her assault continued into his breached cavity. She recruited her accompanied limb to join assault point.

Dread silence ensued. Paralyzed he became. Her chemical inducements expanded and contracted his inner anatomy until no further response from him subsisted. He was not yet dead, but such darkness was inevitable. She wanted to see his face, trapped as it was in such circumstance.

She ripped one tentacle through his chest cavity and moved it in groping form towards and onto his head, lightly circled it, then retracted upon his outward skin form. His head slowly moved around, not killing him yet, as his anatomy allowed for owl-like, near complete rear point reversal. Swivel point limit achieved; she allowed her true facial form to emerge from her hominoid structure disguise.

They gazed upon each other, she in her post-stress comfort, and he in panic state of knowing imminent extinction.

"Chit for your thoughts," she voiced as rough scratch approximation of his auditory capabilities, revealed her sounds impacted his sensations.

"What is your name?"

"My name is Ariadne."

Multiple eyes protruded from his face. Spider eyes, she thought. Part insect he was. Cellophane thin and transparent, long, bluish veined wings attempted twitters as they began to show from his back. She used another tentacle, ripped his shirt to perform more proper study. His head looked down upon scene visited upon his body and what remained intact of it. She began to realize he would not die right away, but near lifeless he was, beyond point of absolute return or regeneration, at least based upon her recall of Training Materials information.

She could not bring herself to finish him off further. If memories still calculated through his brain, perhaps some remorseful state would rush over him. Did not matter. Just observation requirements, she told herself. She wondered if he was transmitting this experience to another, an unseen entity able to record her methods, as education of those in his species to learn from.

His outer appearance mimicked an interpretation by her of dream state similar in most humanoid populations. Her last activity involved extraction of biological material, which had been ongoing since their first contact. She noticed duplication of data in her analytical brain but was able to extract some nuances previously not found, perhaps indication of fluids released as defense mechanism, to ward off pain, anxiety, repair lethally damaged anatomical framework. Almost proud she was when realized some segment of her own activity created in this creature such biological activity during final phases of life.

She, too, searched for chemical or biological evidence of Boymore. Found evidence of many angiosperm seeds, then extracted them from different internal orifices. Quick analysis determined possible Boymore biology seeds, especially "unknowns".

She understood further analysis required. "Thank gods," she stammered into air. Collected seeds, categorized, stored into her designated bio pockets. Hope reigned. Back to business.

Such Target created state was not her intention, nor was creation of torture for him. Observation time of his dream state, that he could now never escape, perhaps allowed him to capture more evil thoughts and mechanisms as survival stimulus; or could be blown synapses in nearly obliterated sentient organism structure; or disparate knowledge capture before imminent drain into murky sewer graves of prior humanoids she killed.

Unable to classify his biology as either humanoid or other such type creature, or insectoid, adiantoid, although some metabolic signs of plant structure presented itself in data chart, she stored all elements for further research. Gomwind and Oni mix present, plus undocumented culture ethnicity per initial analysis. Programmed herself to download entire anatomy and biology designs of accumulated Target Hits.

She looked one last time at remnants of Anton's face. Death smile. He wore it well. She freed him from her physical clutches and prepped for return to her new abode. There would she download all obtained data and return it to her planetoid in same manner as her own arrival.

She remembered last piece of advice granted to her by Overseer: if you do this, Fold, stuck there for long time, are you. Her inner essence was lethal if emitted, but somewhat uncontrollable. She had yet to meet souls who, in her home environment, could be designated redeemable.

She began Fold into systemic origin elements. To Fold

was dangerous as it encompassed all living things within Fold parameters. Boxed into decision of dread pain survival or miserable end, she ceded to Fold.

Her outer skin boundaries receded gradually from head to toe. Her essence flowed like torrents, beautiful in appearance, entrancing, which was part of purpose, yet lethal for any entity captured in flowing snares. Her victim now captured in her unfolding from inside to out, his skin peeled banana-like. Absorption of Anton's biological essence now complete.

Turned on her in-vision Monitors; observed for effectiveness. As her physical being floated to outer boundaries of town, her essence swept up all along travel and touch paths. Ground shimmied, then shook long. Buildings tilted, swayed, crumbled from within. Small creatures in alleys, bushes, sewers began evacuation, yet some captured by telepathic wavelengths and exploded. Struggled, she did, to control destruction. Unable to stop it.

She gained control of one brain wave and sent it directly to Gomwind Magistrate friend. He responded, in kind, to her assistance plea for non-prisoner personnel Evacuation. He slowed Time wave for more effective Evac. "Movements to safety commenced."

She further tried to stop inadvertent destructive wavelengths, but her energy levels, mostly spent on capture and disassembly of Anton, failed to desist. Such destruction not her intention. Then she realized Anton must have infected her. His biology invaded her sensory organs, somewhat controlled her telepathic wavelengths, exploded from her own physical anatomy.

Many small living organisms unable to survive;

either burned, obliterated, melted, remolded, misshaped, squashed, from different perspectives of each entity; either inside out or reverse; front to back; up or down. Any living creature still sentient and within her range of evidence cleanup was bombarded by boney spicules of dust shaken from her inner core, essentially, obliterated by her waste particles. Bio capture sacs remained intact and secure.

Anton's origin point of her essence invasion determined beginning of ending. "I'm not dead yet," she thought, uncertain whether it was actually his thought which had invaded her minds. She tried to center herself, gain control. Searched Memory banks to distract hostile random wavelengths.

Category: Ariadne

Result: No findings.

She tried again. She remembered her Trainer, Flux, called her little Failsafe once, when she was in Training, and had completed physical skill Test combined with Intelligence test at surprisingly high level for her Training Stage. She later heard Flux had been severely scolded by Management for using such nickname. After that scolding, Flux caller her "Teek".

Subset: Failsafe

Ariadne was surprised at noise blast Failsafe subset created from Education system. She aborted screen immediately.

Ariadne existed as experimental being in demon world, of her known Dimension, exported so many times through Dimensions, that when previous Dimensions suffered destruction in wars, no records existed of her presence there. Periphery element, she had become, one of last surviving Failsafe ethnic groups to remain known extant.

Old Earth humanoid historical records indicated world destruction cause accidental, by severe asteroid and meteorite bombardment over short time period, due to change in gravitational waves caused by Quasar explosion.

Sentient Beings not yet catalogued in historical records, who controlled some artificial Quasars, had mistakenly pointed one in wrong direction, causing it to destroy Old Earth. Quasar collected and projected all nearby meteors and asteroids to project into planet gravitational path.

Sentient Beings on Pluto, Uranus, Neptune, Jupiter, Saturn, Mars, Venus and Mercury unempowered to stop extinction. In turn, domino extinction effect evolved. Jupiter societies arranged rescue efforts and temporary sanctuary. Small group of humanoids and biome systems granted rescue from each planet, including Old Earth. All collected species then transported to compatible survival Dimension domains.

Failsafe option evolved to avoid future similar incident. Experiments commenced, biologically and chemically using cells of all known Solar Systems' cultures in order to create Protective class. Over time, Protective Class humanoids not permitted to breed with other Classes, as intelligence and reason and free will were qualities reserved only in Ruling Class biology. Protective Class served only to defend against aggressions pressed by intolerant Resistance Cultures. Barriers breakers punished unmercifully.

Ariadne's culture evolved into Protection Class, bred to protect other Classes of culture and intelligence, and in way, she was expendable, as intelligence was prized over physical skill. But physical skill Classes temporarily took over by sheer force during Quasar Wars, giving some credence to myth that initial Quasar accident indicated intentional act, when much of Intelligence Class, subset of Ruling Class, suffered destruction, although not complete in that regard.

Zero created Classes demonstrated complete honorable mannerisms or intentions, which in some way, allowed by default, permitted survival to trump honor when necessary. Still, Intelligence Class sustained punishment if honor exceptions remained inviolate. Envy, greed, and power acquisition means persisted in all humanoid and otherwise sentient creature etiological systems.

Primary method of controlling Dimensions and worlds therein was Memory Erase. It remained allowed as long as complete memory mechanism not lost. Reprogramming less aggravated sensibilities of humanoid and creature moralities, and thus became incorporated into many cultural systems. Binding thread, if not in practice, at least in theory. Theory trumped practice in Ruling Class. To express such thought punishable by extermination.

Ariadne now resided in Protective Class

Dimension, and her job was Button Hand. Note, Button Hands can also become Mission Targets for other Dimension worlds. Targets chosen pursuant to committed crimes, including moral code violations, treason, or whatever indiscretion Ruling Class drummed up to retain their power.

Suddenly, she realized no control over her own thoughts. Her rumination origin point came from another being. It was Anton. He succeeded in his last moments of attempted resurrection. Anton's soliloquy neared its end.

Ariadne shaken by such exposition of thoughts, froze in physiological and biological trance. Anton had captured her telepathic wave and sent signals to it from his current status of near-death. She tested her premise in question wavelength emitted to him.

"Why tell me these things?"

"Because it created much more interesting skill level confrontation."

She stammered out another wave.

"Then, I must thank you."

"Oh, you don't even know."

She realized too late now. Retreat not possible. Anton's wave persisted.

"When your Management finds out about your skill, they will hide you away, in stasis, for eons, unless desperately needed. You are diamond pretty to show but fears of their own power loss rule them first and foremost; simple insidious infection, these greed and envy emotions."

"In other words, I will be punished, for excess physical skill and intelligence."

"Precisely. You are threat to anyone and everyone, particularly in intelligence."

"So, I'm doomed."

"Precisely. Some of Management would rather die trying to reach your level, and risk Dimensional extinction event, rather than to concede you are their better of Warrior in body, and Analyzer in mind."

"So sad, this situation sounds."

"Yes. Worst part is that I will not die. Before I was sent here, my DNA was harvested and saved. Sometime in future, when necessary, my Dimension Controllers will reactivate me through DNA replication into exact same being, except enhanced by data developed and transmitted to them about my physical and intellectual DNA enhancements developed during this Mission."

"Perhaps, then, we will meet again, in our enhanced states,

in whispers of Angels," she murmured.

"Damn Angels. If you only knew," he exhaled in sighs.

No audible sounds now. No linguistic puffery. No insults. No threats. Sense bizarre of future calling swirled rough inside her gut. Wavelength brains hum lost.

His silence disturbed her. His wave disconnected. Her body toxins she released into Anton's collected biological elements, then slowly poisoned him in all aspects of his anatomy. His essence stung at her, repeatedly. Her squirms and tentacle flails could not loosen from his ephemeral grip. Eventually, pain spasms halted.

As for remainders of sentient life in Prison colony, only inanimate objects still existed like buildings, sidewalk, as her body chemistry automatically made decisions of worthy or unworthy for continued contributions to greater society.

All living things were captured by Fold, except for Gomwinds and those rescued by Gomwinds, and two more: Ariadne . . . and her youngling victim acquaintance, Boymore.

In time, she and Boymore would become re-born in flowering Era of uncertain Spring's future. Her, as bloom into her next sentient self for Mission Task continuance, subject to Management approval; and youngling little Boymore, to serve her as Apprentice-in-training, if Management approved.

Ariadne looked into collection of Mission Target biology essence packets; spied Anton's compacted remains; cupped her hands; created small dirt mound; pressed upon it like raw meatloaf. Mouthed blessing kind.

"I don't know where I am going, I must say. I hope to see you again someday."

She wondered if her male adversary rested merely in some unknown stasis form, awaiting rejuvenation. Quickly such thought escaped her mind, as if it had never been there. Just as soon, thoughts flooded her head from her last Mission Training sequence. Revenge exuded musky odor, but it certainly burnt sweet tongue taste, in rumination.

Source: Controller Cloud

Data Extract: SBHC-Sentient Being History of the Cosmos

Subset Category: Tipping point exists in all actions

Freedoms:

to rest, to resist, to recalculate, to err and correct, expression, repression, action, inaction, aspire, retire, enjoy, critique

7 baneful (harmful or destructive) character flaws:

1 Self-doubt; many times, knotted to a failure; goals, like rules, are made to be broken and then reformed into stronger compound; humanoids and civilizations derived therefrom cannot escape such path.

2 Regret without self-apology and renewal; sometimes learning from mistakes is difficult because learning is difficult step along path of advanced knowledge; mistakes

are easier to repeat than avoid through learning new or

better or more efficient or productive path.

3 Second-guessing is like living with window blinds always drawn closed; need to open them up to see present and imagine future.

4 Living in past; rehashing mentally past experiences may help cleanse one's conscience, but then time comes to step out of such prison and embark into present and further; what has happened is over and can't be relived except in imagination; to reside only in imagination is to exist outside present reality, where all things happen.

5 Dreaming and not doing, i.e. imagining better days but

no steps taken, and no plan created to achieve better days.

6 Wanting too much what others have, to level where no appreciation derived from what one has gained or accomplished.

7 Giving up, i.e. unwilling to take stock of oneself, daring to start over and striving to continue anew.

Conclusion

Each day unveiled unique world of its own, from beginning to end; so much to explore, attempt, fail, accomplish, try and re-try while traveling across sometimes smooth, sometimes rocky or pothole marked roads and paths. Cities not built in one day; neither were day cities' alone. Day was not owned by city; it was owned by everyone residing there and around there.

Democracy, envisioned as jewel of sentient existence for individual spirit; no government can own such jewel, or possess it, absent mining and polishing of Beings who discovered and owned it. No nation or village or hamlet existed absent will of individuals who formed it.

One's will never became totally crushed by those entrusted to keep safe such jewel. No propaganda or communication thereof by surrogates could mask or eliminate soul of individual. That soul and spirit beamed as Universe master.

Machines, like humanoids, lasted longer when they were not used to point of exhaustion.

"In tonight's air, something's there." Her own epitaph she sang.

"Find wisdom in every soul. Only way ... to reach ... Destination."

Her mind wandered more. Wanted more. But

wander ruled now. Just kept doing. Moving. More, more, more. Never enough. No rest satisfied. To be remembered for things done, spoken, she yearned for. Not allowed in her world. Erroneously, most likely, her thoughts tortured, poked. She rolled Boymore biome remains into Evac tube.

Filtered were these actions physical and verbal, by perspective bias of those not aware of such penitential acerbations. Morning begged release. Her dormancy time, and that of her new and secret prodigy, Boymore, beckoned. She rolled herself into biome Evac tube.

Last Breath. "Don't leave me, thoughts. Don't leave."

Her thoughts thrashed for more meaning.

"Hello. I must be going."

No more movement. Sleep. Sleep in peace, Ariadne. No dreams. No nightmares. No tortured memory moments.

10

9

Word of Mission results traveled fast among Nazranians. Flux contemplated Ariadne's Mission. Die now. Live later. She was as done as done could be created in this Mission. Her lack of perfection was perfection itself. Became flower which evolved through growth, decay, death cycle. Time frame determined by next Mission activation status.

At Mission start time, her seeds would be strewn by winds which caused them to cling onto moving objects that could take them many geographical places. Trucks, cars, boats, ships, animals, insects, flowered species, even humanoids would unwittingly become her accomplices, only for growth allowance again, so she could start over.

Regret forget offered chance to redo and re-

remember again. Déjà vu, of sister Memory sewn deep into her milt, birthed views worth remembering. Simple things retracted into hiding; spiders of deceit; hungry colors; killers of defeat.

From Universes evolved small points.

Chronicler First Draft Submission, Complete

11

Final Evaluation, notes from Controller

"Ariadne demonstrates remarkable skills for entry-Level Button Hand first assignment start. Skills comparable to Assassins rated 2 levels higher. In effect, overachieved, completed all Mission Tasks, plus eliminated one highly skilled demon Assassin threat from another Dimension which we just started to explore not long ago. My concern is Ariadne may become overconfident, allowing skills to erode into regression status nurtured by potential vanity issues. Such condition cannot be tolerated.

xxx (Commentary classified. New data developed, unknown previously, limited to Level 8 eyes or higher) xxx.

Average rating reflects my professional concerns,

after Overseer discussion (notes attached), and thus will result in future Training efforts to prevent such weakness development. Ariadne will be counseled as caution against anticipated regression. Assignment completed. Regrets minimal."

Report Summary, Ordinator 5

Review Status Restrictions: Level 7 or higher.

Mission Status: Completed.

Availability Status: Regeneration in progress.

Controller Review: Completed.

Overseer Review: Referenced. Catalogued.

Counseling Recommendations:

No ___

Yes _X_

NA ___

If you enjoyed this book, do not forget to leave a review on Amazon!

I highly appreciate your reviews, and it only takes a minute to do.

Mike Gutowski is a retired insurance investigator, and now self-employed author of horror, science fiction, dark fantasy and dystopian fantasy books. Inspired by 3 adult daughters, Baltimore life, travels to several states along East Coast USA and in the Heartland. There are stories everywhere; just have to listen, see, experience long enough to somehow bake a twisted sense of it all.

www.ingramcontent.com/pod-product-compliance
Lightning Source LLC
Chambersburg PA
CBHW071434100726
47908CB00004B/1157